EDITED BY
DAVID DREVER AND LIAM STEWART

The Other Side
of the Clyde

PUFFIN BOOKS

Puffin Books, Penguin Books Ltd, Harmondsworth, Middlesex, England
Viking Penguin Inc., 40 West 23rd Street, New York, New York 10010, U.S.A.
Penguin Books Australia Ltd, Ringwood, Victoria, Australia
Penguin Books Canada Limited, 2801 John Street, Markham, Ontario, Canada L3R 1B4
Penguin Books (N.Z.) Ltd, 182–190 Wairau Road, Auckland 10, New Zealand

This collection first published 1986

Made and printed in Great Britain by
Hazell Watson & Viney Ltd,
Member of the BPCC Group,
Aylesbury, Bucks
Filmset in Linotron Sabon by
Rowland Phototypesetting Ltd
Bury St Edmunds, Suffolk

arRon

PUFFIN PLUS

The Other Side of the Clyde

Two boys on a daring voyage of discovery across the Clyde; the trials and tribulations of a new boy at school; the lament of a fat girl – these are just a few of the fascinating characters who come alive in this vibrant new collection of writing from Scotland. Drawn from both new and established writers, this book offers humour and dry wit, wishful longing, the sadness of lost innocence, stark reality and some poetry of the finest quality.

There is much excellent writing coming from Scotland at this time. Here is just some of the best, gathered together especially for older readers.

David Drever and Liam Stewart are both Glaswegians educated at Glasgow University. David Drever now teaches English and Liam Stewart is a tutor in WEA writers' workshops. Both are married with children.

Contents

5

Introduction

Two boys cross the Clyde, hoping to find a new world of adventure and excitement; a Glasgow youth is drawn to Belfast after a visit from his uncle, an IRA hero; a shocking childhood experience puts a boy off rhubarb for the rest of his life; a posh girl from the suburbs enters the life of an unemployed boy from a housing estate; school term opens with the prospect of having to face the dreaded McGunnigle once again; Oor Hamlet kills his stepfather; a fat girl confesses; *Top of the Pops* counts down to its last ever number one . . .

These stories and poems are mainly about the people of Glasgow and its nearby towns and countryside. A few take place in the past, dealing with a way of life that is now gone. Most of them are happening today. Like all cities, Glasgow has a personality of its own, which is best observed when its people talk. The people in the following pages speak in their everyday language – words that are sometimes strange, but are also very real. They are poems and stories about ordinary people at extraordinary times in their lives. We hope they say something to you and, above all, we hope you find them good reading.

Liam Stewart
David Drever

The Ferry

ALAN SPENCE

The cane arrow rose in the still warm air. Aleck and Joe shielded their eyes from the sun and watched its flight. It seemed to rise, clear of the tenements that enclosed them and hang for a moment against the sky before turning back to complete its arc and fall to land with a jar that staved and shuddered its whole length on the hardpacked dirt and brick of the back court.

'It's a goodyin!' said Joe, grinning and flexing the bow that Aleck had just made. The bow had fired its first shot, and it was good. Aleck nodded and set about making a bow for himself as Joe ran across to pick up the arrow.

They had bought six bits of bamboo cane. Each was long enough to make a bow or be broken in half to make two arrows.

Aleck was stringing the bows, notching each end for the string to fit, and Joe was making the arrows. If he had simply snapped the canes in half the pieces would have split, leaving each arrow a loose mess of fibres and split ends. So he used an old hacksaw blade to cut carefully through each cane before breaking it and binding each end with black insulating tape.

They played at their craft with seriousness. They were crouched in a clearing. The grey buildings were their jungle and the fragments of stone and broken glass they had gathered and laid out were imagined arrowheads of flint and bone.

The hacksaw blade cutting through the cane sometimes made a harsh rasping noise that set Aleck's teeth on edge. Like the squeak of polystyrene rubbed on a window. Like the scrape and squeal of the teacher's chalk on the blackboard.

(Guide-lines for her chalk against the black – like the lines on the pages of his jotter – date in the left-hand margin – NAME in the middle of the top line – below that (miss two lines) the title of the composition – 'What I want to be' – sun shafting in through the window, lighting on dancing particles of dust – dust of chalk in the air – sunlight – what I want – to be.)

At the beginning of the long summer holidays it had seemed as if they could never end. Eight weeks was an eternity stretching before them. Now, incredibly, five of those precious weeks had passed.

'Imagine huvin tae go back tae school 'n a cuppla weeks,' said Aleck.

'You're no sa bad,' said Joe. 'Youse Proddies uv goat a week merr than us.'

'Ach well,' said Aleck. 'Youse ur always gettin hoalidays a obligation. Jist wan saint efter another. Ah think we should get an extra two weeks tae make up fur it.'

Joe stuck out his tongue and gave Aleck the V-sign. Then he grinned.

'Heh Aleck, comin wull no bother gawn back tae school? Wull jist run away an dog it forever.'

'That wid be brilliant!' said Aleck. 'Wherr could we go?'

Joe held up his arrow.

'We could go tae America an live wi REAL Indians. Ah've goat an auntie in Canada.'

'Ach thur's nae real Indians left,' said Aleck. 'They aw get pit oot 'n daft wee reservations.'

'How aboot India then?' said Joe. 'Or Africa? We could live in a tree hoose.'

'Pick bananas 'n oranges,' said Aleck.

'Hunt animals.'

'Make pals wi some a them but,' said Aleck. 'Lions 'n tigers an that.'

'Great white chiefs. Me chief Joseph.' He pouted his lips and spoke in as deep a voice as he could, beating his chest with his fist.

'Me chief Alexander,' said Aleck, raising his bow. 'We wid huv tae gie wursels better names but.'

'Walla Walla Wooski!' said Joe.

'We could paint wursels tae,' said Aleck. 'Werr feathers an bones.'

'Imagine bein cannibals,' said Joe. 'We could jist eat white men that got loast in the jungle.'

'Fancy gawn intae the chippy,' said Aleck, 'an askin fur two single fish an a whiteman supper!'

(Louie in the chip shop – like Sweeney Todd – cutting people up for pies – rubbing his hands and gloating over the carcass of a fat schoolboy – ambushed in the back court.)

'People ur supposed tae taste like pork,' Aleck said at last. 'Think ah'll stoap eatin meat.'

'Ach don't be daft,' said Joe. 'If we didnae eat animals we'd get ett wursels.'

'Suppose so,' said Aleck.

He put the finishing touches to his bow. Joe taped the last arrowhead. They went padding off across Congos and Zambezis of their own making, to see what was to be hunted.

Aleck lay with his eyes closed on the flat roof of the midden, the warmth of the sun on his bare arms and legs, his face against the stone. And nothing existed outside himself in that moment. (Colour, mainly red, behind his eyes – warm, warm – low sounds, a feeling, a murmur – flies, drone – voices far away – a dream, faint breeze – laughter, a car, tin can dropped in a bin – warm, he lay like some great slow lizard, coiled and lazing on a warm rock – he could almost remember it.)

He sat up suddenly and looked around. The colours were still behind his eyes. He focused on Joe on the ground below, stalking a pigeon. Joe. The back court. Hunting. It was real. He was Aleck. His whole life had actually happened.

Joe shot his arrow and the pigeon flustered off to circle round and perch on a railing.

'Bastard!' said Joe.

The arrow skimmed the wall where the pigeon had sat and landed on the other side in the next back court.

'Gonnae nik doon an get that Aleck?' said Joe, looking up.

From his high perch on the dyke Aleck could see both back courts.

'Ther's some fullas watchin yer doo,' he said. 'Thu'll prob'ly huv the perry us fur tryin tae shoot it.'

Aleck climbed down on to the wall.

'If ye hear me gettin mangled yull know whit's happened,' he said.

'Ach well,' said Joe, 'it wis nice knowin ye.'

Aleck dropped down on to the other side of the wall.

The men gave no sign that they had even noticed him but he hesitated to move for the arrow, which had landed almost at their feet.

It was funny to think of them as bird-watchers. Most of them were in their twenties or thirties, one or two were older. Men without jobs who seemed to spend their whole time loafing or shambling around, always in a cluster, scuffling and shabby, always finding ways to fill the time till the glorious weekend when there was money for wine and they were loud and alive and glowing, singing and fighting and sick.

Watching the pigeons was a mystery with its secrets, its initiates, a language of its own. They would cup their hands to their mouths and echo the bird's own call. They used strange words like fantail and others that Aleck could never quite make out or understand. Some of them even built wooden doocots, box-hutches where the birds could feed. Doocot meant dovecot because doo was short for dove. Dovecot. Cot for a dove. But the pigeons were mostly grey, although if you could look closely you might see colours. Like an oil stain on the road under the light. Gurgling and strutting and grey. Doves should be soft and graceful and white. Like the dove sent from the ark, to find land where it could rest. Miss Riddie had told them the story and taught them the song.

(The words chalked on the blackboard – teacher with her pointer – repeat after me –

> O that I had wings like a dove
> Then I would fly away and be at rest
> Lo then would I wander far off
> And remain in the wilderness

di dum diddy dum diddy dum / diddy dum diddy dum didum.)

One of the men picked up the arrow. He looked straight at Aleck and snapped the arrow in two. He was grinning.

'Aw. . .izzat no a shame. . .ah've went an broke it!'

The others laughed and he threw the pieces aside.

'Get tae buggery wi yer bows 'n arras or ah'll snap yer bloody neck!'

Aleck ran and scrambled back across the wall.

The pigeon rose and soared over the rooftops and out of sight.

The afternoon sticky and hot and the pavement tar soft and melting. Aleck and Joe were scraping their initials with their arrows.

(The way the tar opened under the pressure – glistening black scar on the pavement's dusty grey – initials – names.)

'Tar's brilliant stuff, intit,' said Joe.

'So it is,' said Aleck. 'See the smell aff it when its jist been laid! Makes ye wanty sink yer teeth inty it!'

'So it dis. Ah love smells lik that.'

'The smell a the subway!'

'New shoe boaxes!'

'Rubber tyres!'

'Terrific!'

Joe dug into the tar, wound the arrow till its end was coiled and clogged.

'Looks like a big toly disn't it!'

They dug out lumps with their hands, kneaded and stretched and smeared it.

'Really dis make ye wanty eat it.'

'D'you remember eatin sand when ye wur wee?' asked Aleck.

'Naw, ah don't think so,' said Joe. 'How, d'you?'

'Aye. Sandpies it wis. Looked great. Tasted horrible but.'

(Mouthful of dirt – becoming mud – grit between the teeth.)

'Jesus!' said Joe. 'How ur we gonnae get this stuff aff?'

Aleck looked at his blackened hands. 'Margarine's supposed tae take it aff,' he said.

'We could always leave them,' said Joe. 'Cover wursels in it.'

'Fur gawn tae the jungle,' said Aleck. He picked up his bow and arrows.

'Ach look at that!' said Joe. His arrow had split digging into the tar. He threw it away, disgusted.

'Never mind,' said Aleck. ''Mon wull go up tae mah hoose'n clean it aff.'

Margarine smeared on their tarry hands, a greasy mess, the fat and the tar merging to make a mucky green as they rubbed and scraped and tried to clean it off.

'Horrible, intit?' said Joe, looking at his hands.

'Imagine seein thaym comin ower yer shooder'n a dark night,' said Aleck. He wailed and thrust gnarled slimy claws towards Joe. They stalked each other round the kitchen, menacing the furniture with green and trembling werewolf paws.

'Smelly,' said Aleck, stopping in mid-growl to sniff his hands. He went to the sink and tried washing them clean under the tap but the cold water couldn't dissolve the grease which still clung in globules and streaks.

'Ah canny really be bothered bilin up a kettle a watter,' he said.

'Gie's up that auld towel aff the flerr, wull ye?'

With the towel they managed to rub off most of the dirt.

''At's no bad,' said Joe. 'Prob'ly werr aff in a day ur two.'

They looked at the dirt still ingrained in the skin and under their nails.

'Dead quiet,' said Joe, unaccustomed to the emptiness of the house. Joe had brothers and sisters and his house was always loud with their noise.

'Suppose so,' said Aleck.

The tick of the clock. Stillness. Noises from the back court.

'Think ah'll jist stey in,' said Aleck. 'That's hauf four the noo, an ma mammy'll be hame fae ur work at five.'

'When dis yer da get in?' asked Joe.

'Aboot hauf five ur somethin.'

Joe lifted his bow and moved towards the door.

'Fancy gin doon tae the ferry efter tea?' he said.

'The ferry?'

'Aye, we could nik acroass tae Partick an play aboot therr 'nen come back. Disnae cost anythin.'

'At's a great idea,' said Aleck. 'See ye efter tea then.'

He handed Joe one of his arrows.

'Here,' he said. 'That's us git wan each.'

Past a pub with a cluster of neon grapes above the door, past a mission hall called Bethel, left off Govan Road and along a narrow lane, through the docks to the ferry steps.

Ferry steps. They were often invoked as part of a prophecy, against the drunk and incapable. Spat out like a curse – 'That yin'll finish up at the fit a the ferry steps.'

Aleck and Joe sat at the top of the steep slippery wooden steps, waiting for the ferry to cross from the Partick side.

'Imagine slippin fae here,' said Joe. 'Ye'd jist tummel right in.'

They looked in silence, down to where the steps disappeared into black invisible depth, the oily river lapping softly.

'Here it comes!' said Aleck.

They stood up and watched as the squat brown ferry chugged across towards them.

The water swirled up the steps as it bumped and thudded to rest.

The ferry had the same kind of low dumpy bulk as a tug, though it was much smaller. It had a long low deck with sides to a height of about three feet running along its whole length and open at each end. Spanning the middle section was a canopy. This gave shelter for the passengers in the rain and also covered the pilot's wheel-house. The whole ferry, including the canopy, was painted the same dull brown.

Aleck and Joe went to the front and leaned over the side. Smoke phutted from the chimney as the ferry chugged its way out. Joe had left his bow at home but Aleck had brought his with him, the one remaining arrow tucked under his belt. He trailed the bow in the water, watching the wake ripple out behind it, the boat rocking gently beneath them, the feel of the deck through their thin-soled shoes.

Towering along both banks were the great jutting cranes of the shipyards, a tanker further downstream, gulls circling overhead.

They'd been told a little about the river in school. How it began as a trickle away in the southern uplands and wound its way down through sheep farms and mining towns and eventually flowed through Glasgow and beyond to the firth and the open sea.

'Funny tae think'n aw this watter comin fae a wee stream up'n the hills,' said Aleck.

'Intit,' said Joe.

'Ah mean, the same watter,' said Aleck.

They were silent, looking down at the oily flow. Grey with colours. Like the pigeon.

The journey was too quickly over. At the Partick side they

charged up the steps then stopped and looked around them. The ferry started back across.

Miss Riddie had told them about Partick and Govan growing side by side. The deepening of the river. Shipbuilding. Cheap houses for the shipyard workers. She had said they were like reflections, Partick and Govan, with the river like a mirror in between.

The grey buildings looked the same, but they were not their own. They felt lost and threatened. The strange streets and unfamiliar faces were hostile. At the corner opposite, a group of men loafing. Boys their own age, playing, looking towards them. They would have to go past them to get clear of the ferry.

'D'you know anywherr tae go?' asked Aleck.

'Naw. No really,' said Joe.

'D'ye fancy jist gawn back?'

'Comin?'

'Right, c'mon!'

They squatted on the steps waiting. If Partick and Govan were on opposite sides of the mirror, only one side was real. It depended on where you had been brought up. And for Aleck and Joe, Govan was the only reality they knew. When they were back once more on the steps at the Govan side, Joe turned to Aleck.

'Heh! D'ye fancy jist steyin oan the ferry an gawn back an furrat a coupla times? Jist fur a wee hurl?'

'At's a great idea!' said Aleck. They jumped back on to the ferry just in time before it moved off.

The low sun was bright on the water and the shadows it cast were long. 'Heh Aleck,' said Joe. 'Ye could haud up the driver wi yer bow'n arra an get um tae take us tae America or Africa or wherrever it wis.'

'Imagine!' said Aleck. He looked at the bow. 'Och wid ye

lookit the state ae it!' The string had split the cane at one end and the split had continued half-way down its length.

'Never mind,' said Joe.

'Disnae really matter, ah suppose.'

At the Partick side they decided to jump off and join the oncoming passengers for the journey back, just for the sake of the leap from the deck to the steps. But when they tried to get back on the pilot blocked their way.

'Right!' he said. 'Yizzur steyin aff. Yizzuv bin up an doon aff this boat lik a bloody yoyo. D'ye think it's jist fur playin oan? Noo goan! Get!'

They stood helpless, watching as the ferry moved off towards their home shore.

'Whit'll we dae noo?' asked Aleck.

'There's another ferry up at the Art Galleries,' said Joe. 'We could walk it up.'

'Wull that no take us a while?' said Aleck.

'Nothin else we kin dae.' Joe looked out after the ferry, now almost at the Govan side.

'Bastard!' he said.

Aleck threw his split bow and his last arrow into the water and watched them being swirled out by the current. He wondered how far they would be carried. Out past the shipyards, past Greenock and Gourock to the firth, past the islands, out past Ireland, out to the Atlantic, out . . .

Aleck suddenly shivered. The sky was beginning to darken. The river was deep and wide. They were far from home, in an alien land.

'Bloody Partick,' said Joe.

They began the slow climb to the top of the ferry steps.

Moral Philosophy

TOM LEONARD

whiji *mean* whiji mean

lissn
noo lissnty mi toknty yi
right

h hawd oan
whair wuzza
naw

aye
whitsiz name
him way thi
yi no yon

here
here yoo
yir no eevn lissnin
name a god

a doant no

Washing the Coins

DOUGLAS DUNN

You'd start at seven, and then you'd bend your back
Until they let you stand up straight, your hands
Pressed on your kidneys as you groaned for lunch,
Thick sandwiches in grease-proofed bundles, piled
Beside the jackets by the hawthorn hedges.
And then you'd bend your little back again
Until they let you stand up straight. Your hands,
On which the earth had dried in layers, itched, itched,
Though worse still was that ache along the tips
Of every picking finger, each broken nail
That scraped the ground for sprawled potatoes
The turning digger churned out of the drills.
Muttering strong Irish men and women worked
Quicker than local boys. You had to watch them.
They had the trick of sideways-bolted spuds
Fast to your ear, and the upset wire basket
That broke your heart but made the Irish laugh.
You moaned, complained, and learned the rules of work.
Your boots, enlarging as the day wore on,
Were weighted by the magnets of the earth,
And rain in the face was also to have
Something in common with bedraggled Irish.
You held your hands into the rain, then watched
Brown water drip along your chilling fingers
Until you saw the colour of your skin

Through rips disfiguring your gloves of mud.
It was the same for everyone. All day
That bead of sweat tickled your smeared nose
And a glance upwards would show you trees and clouds
In turbulent collusions of the sky
With ground and ground with sky, and you portrayed
Among the wretched of the native earth.
Towards the end you felt you understood
The happy rancour of the Irish howkers.
When dusk came down, you stood beside the byre
For the farmer's wife to pay the labour off.
And this is what I remember by the dark
Whitewash of the byre wall among shuffling boots.
She knew me, but she couldn't tell my face
From an Irish boy's, and she apologized
And roughed my hair as into my cupped hands
She poured a dozen pennies of the realm
And placed two florins there, then cupped her hands
Around my hands, like praying together.
It is not good to feel you have no future.
My clotted hands turned coins to muddy copper.
I tumbled all my coins upon our table.
My mother ran a basin of hot water.
We bathed my wages and we scrubbed them clean.
Once all that sediment was washed away,
That residue of field caked on my money,
I filled the basin to its brim with cold;
And when the water settled I could see
Two English kings among their drowned Britannias.

Blood

KEITH AITCHISON

It was a sunny week in late August, when the heat curled along the streets and up the tenement stairs of the baker's oven of a city, that Timothy Maguire came to stay with his widowed sister and his nephew.

'By God, have I not brought the good weather with me!' he exclaimed, putting down his suitcase and beaming at them, his round face shining with sweat.

'Mary!' he embraced his sister, then thrust out his hand. 'And this hulking giant cannot be young Martin?'

'I'm nineteen, Uncle Tim.' Martin's hand was gripped.

'Nineteen, is it?' Timothy whistled. 'By God, there's time passed, and a lot of Maguire grown in this lad, Mary. Does he not look like our father when young?'

'He has the eyes, just. The face is his own father's. Come, sit down.'

Timothy sat and pulled out a handkerchief to mop his face and the wet, darkened roots of his fair hair. 'And how is it with you both?' he asked.

'Martin grows up, and I grow older,' said Mary, and plucked at a lock of her hair. 'Do you see the grey?'

'No more than before.'

'That was four years ago. The funeral.'

'Ah, I meant to come sooner. But business, and other things. You should have come to me for a time.'

'I don't think Belfast is the place for holidays now.'

'Maybe not. It's remarkable how you get accustomed to it all, though,' Timothy paused. 'And it's not as if the cause were not just.'

'The cause!' Mary shook her head. 'You're the son of your father, right enough.'

'And proud of it,' Timothy smiled. 'Was he not a great man after all?'

'What cause?' Martin interjected, curious.

'You don't know?' Timothy stared in amazement, round eyes in a round face.

'That's enough.' Mary rose sharply, and Timothy thought that right enough the years and the widowing had taken more from her than she deserved to lose.

'What cause?' asked Martin once more. 'Ireland?'

'Ireland! Of course, Ireland,' said Timothy with relief. 'Thank God you've not lost your heritage entirely.'

'Half his heritage, or more likely, remembering mother's opinions, one quarter,' said Mary, going into the scullery and speaking back over her shoulder. 'And remember his father, and his side of the family.'

'Aren't they Irish too, with the name O'Brien?' asked Timothy.

'No one remembers when they came over, but it was long ago. And it's near tea-time.'

'The blood's the same. The years don't change it.'

'Ah, the old blood, who knows who else has got into it over the centuries,' said Mary sourly, 'and bugger the old blood for any argument.'

Martin's jaw dropped at the flaring of his mother's temper. Timothy winked at him and gave a long whistle.

'The language!' he called. 'That's my mother's daughter right enough.'

'Who else would put up with you?' Mary asked back, but her voice was no longer sour.

'Do you remember the time mother lost her temper with that butcher in Foyle Street, the one who sold her the wormy meat?'

They laughed together, good humour restored, and Timothy went to his suitcase and brought out a bottle of Irish whiskey.

'Just an aperitif, as the French say.' He poured three glasses. 'It's a great pity James is not still with us, he loved a good whiskey.'

'He never refused any whiskey, good or bad,' said Mary, with neither malice nor sadness, turning her head to smile at Martin and show she was not serious.

'Well now, Martin.' Timothy watched approvingly as his nephew swallowed the whiskey. 'I'll be looking to you to show me around Glasgow. I don't know it at all.'

'You'll have an advantage then,' said Mary. 'Most who do know it well have had to forget the half of what they know in order to find out where they are.'

'Redevelopment?'

'That's the name they give it, the smart name so that we won't notice the way they've ruined the city.'

'The progress is a great thing for them as makes money from it.'

Martin listened to them talk, hearing them drift back down the years to their shared memories. The talk, the memories and the unaccustomed whiskey had softened the Glasgow in his mother's voice. The more she spoke, the more an underlying Belfast edge cut through in the words, as if an echo from the past.

'Tell me, how's young Mary and her man?' asked Timothy suddenly. 'Do you hear from them at all?'

'I do. They're both well, down there in Leeds, and I'm to visit in October and see their new house.'

'New house?' Timothy whistled. 'They must be doing well. And you, young Martin, are you going to visit your sister?'

'No,' said Martin. 'I hope to have found work by then, or else I'll still be looking for it.'

After they had eaten, and after Timothy had remarked that Mary's cooking was still the best east of home, he followed Martin back down the winding stairs and out into the evening, with the tenement shadow sweeping down in a cooling tide along the length of the street, still pleasantly warm for a stroll in shirt-sleeves, with the children calling and playing around the closemouths of the grey tenements curving towards the heart of the city.

Timothy and Martin strolled along the pavement to the main road, and watched the pedestrians and traffic, the city's people in sunlit evening hours between their day and sleep. The doors of the pubs were opened to any cooling breeze, and the sounds of talk and laughter, the clinking of glasses and bottles breathed out on to the pavements in a warm beery invitation.

'When I was in France,' said Timothy, 'the pubs would have tables on the street, where you could sit on evenings like this and take a cool glass. It's a pity we couldn't do that tonight.'

'We haven't the weather for it,' said Martin apologetically. 'It's not like this very often.'

'Still, it would make a great sight, would it not? The Glasgow topers sitting in the rain outside every pub, with their glasses filling up with water and the waiters in mackintoshes and Wellington boots. People would pay to see that.'

Martin laughed, beginning to warm to his uncle's humour.

'And no soldiers,' Timothy mused, watching a group of young men pass by joking among themselves. 'You don't know how lucky you are, Martin. No soldiers, and nobody afraid.'

'I see it on the television,' said Martin, awkward with the sudden change.

'Your television is censored, I'll tell you that. They don't dare to show you even one half of what the soldiers do, over there.'

Martin shuffled his feet, uncomfortable with this grim note in Timothy.

'Ah well,' Timothy slapped Martin's back. 'Why talk of that now? Your lives aren't touched by it, thank God, and I'm on holiday.'

'And do you see,' he continued, 'how the pubs in this street are positively entreating us to cross their thresholds. Are you a drinking man, now?'

'I take a pint or two,' admitted Martin.

'And two it will be,' said Timothy, and steered his nephew into the nearest pub.

A pint in his fist, Timothy took a long pull and smacked his lips. He looked around the pub with a seasoned eye, noting the long formica bar with plain mirrors behind and the gantries on either side. There were little tables in the corners, and over it all a cloud of cigarette smoke and the hard language of men drinking with no women in the company.

'A man's pub,' Timothy observed. 'You wouldn't be bringing your girlfriends here, Martin?'

'I haven't got one, just now.'

'No? Playing the field, is it?'

'Playing nothing. I've no work, Uncle Tim,' Martin felt ashamed, knowing there was no cause for shame. 'No money, no girlfriend.'

'Just "Tim", eh? I'm your mother's younger brother,' Timothy said, and sighed. 'So, no work and no girl. That's hard. And you'll need the job to get the money to find a girl.'

'I had work. But they laid us off, and it's been the dole for three months.'

'Ah, it's hard. I've been without work myself so I know. I do joinery now, my own boss and it keeps me going.'

Timothy looked around the bar, and the smile returned to his face.

'How do you spend your time?' he asked. 'Do you watch the football?'

'The Celtic.' Martin's chin lifted. 'I go to Parkhead with my mates in the season, when we've got the money. We can't afford the away matches.'

'And tell me, is there that powerful atmosphere we hear about? Songs and the Irish flag waving?'

'Songs and chants,' Martin flushed with the alcohol's gift of enthusiasm. 'When we play Rangers, we do it all specially to annoy the Orangemen. We sing the Soldiers' Song and chant "IRA – all the way!" and all that! It's great!'

'Is it now?' Timothy laughed and emptied his glass. 'Well, that sounds like the sons of Erin to me.'

He stood up to make his way to the bar, counting out money into his hand. Martin started to rise, reaching for the pound notes in his hip pocket.

'I'll get this one.'

'You will not,' Timothy reached out with a work-hardened hand and held him down in his seat. 'These are on me, and no arguments.'

It seemed to Martin as if for once a week passed too

quickly. He spent his days and evenings with Timothy. Once they took the train to Edinburgh, together with Mary, and on another day, a glaring hot day, the three of them went down to Largs and passed the day in sunshine on the sand and in the water. That evening, Timothy took them for dinner in a white-fronted restaurant with ropes looped ship-fashion around the balcony rails, and they ate and drank royally at a white-clothed table looking out at the sea and the hills of Arran.

It seemed to Martin that Timothy had lifted him from the grey drudgery of unemployment, and it was a feeling of gratitude, together with his natural liking for his uncle, that brought them as close and familiar as any friends.

A question of his grandfather began to build in Martin's mind. He had never known him, and somehow the subject had never arisen at home, or perhaps it had been deliberately avoided. As the week passed, with Timothy's presence the vacuum of his mother's Irish family began to fill in patches, like clouds gathering in a clear sky, and subtly altered the way in which Martin saw himself. He remembered Timothy speaking: 'A great man after all,' and curiosity nagged at him with the persistence of toothache, now sharp and demanding, now dull and weak, but always unavoidably claiming his attention, and refusing quiescence.

The night before Timothy left for home, the pair of them travelled to a famously Irish bar on the south side of the city. The evening began to a medley of soft Irish songs played and sung by a blackbrowed accordionist, and later, as the drink flowed both into him and into his audience, and the clouds of cigarette smoke streamed up through the evening to the yellow ceiling, the soft lilts of the Gael gradually made way for the harsher war songs and proud laments of the Fenian men and the IRA. Timothy sang with others in the bar, a mellow baritone in 'Sean South', and even 'The Belfast Brigade', and Martin listened and drank among the other descendants of expatriate Irish, and was swept along on their hazy tides of emotion.

'Tell me about grandfather,' he asked Timothy. 'You said I resemble him.'

Timothy leaned back in his chair and looked at Martin, raising and dropping his eyebrows, crinkling and smoothing his forehead. He sucked the air in through his teeth with a hiss, and expelled it again.

'You don't know,' he said finally. 'Your mother has no regard for him at all; I think she'd be angry if I spoke much of him.'

'Tell me,' Martin's appetite was whetted. 'Tell me! I'll keep quiet, I won't let on anything you say.'

'It's your right to know, maybe,' mused Timothy. 'It's a man's birthright to know the ways of his family. But it's not for me to be telling you. You're your mother's son, not mine.'

'Please!' Martin begged, frantic with drink and curiosity. 'You've got to tell me, can't you see?'

Timothy tapped his glass and listened to the accordionist play a lament for Cathal Brugha. He nodded slowly.

'I will, then. If you don't blab.'

'I won't!'

'It'll be our secret, yes? Between us only?'

'I promise, I promise!' Martin said eagerly.

'Very well' Timothy spoke quietly, beneath the music's insistent notes. 'Your grandfather, my father, Sean Maguire, fought and died for Ireland. The Brits shot him down on a hillside in Fermanagh, and he lies with the heroes in the Republican plot in Armagh.'

Martin felt the impact of each word, opening and shutting

his mouth in amazement. He stared silently at Timothy's serious round face, and knew that this was the truth. His world turned upon itself.

'I never knew,' he managed at last. 'I was never told. Never!'

'Your grandmother had a hard time bringing up us children without a man to provide. She never really forgave father for putting country before family.'

Timothy shrugged, fatalistic at the unchanging strangeness of things.

'You see, Martin,' he continued, 'that's the way women think, that's how they're made. The bitterness rubbed off on Mary, and that's how you never were told at all, I suppose.'

'She should have told me,' Martin said, a note of anger in his voice.

'It's a secret, mind,' Timothy said sharply, a little alarmed. 'Not a word!'

'I promised,' agreed Martin, and began to fill with more questions.

They drank more than on any other night spent together in a bar. Irish whiskey with every pint, and a pint in every half-hour, downed to the note of the accordion and the singing.

Towards closing time, a small old man in a dark jacket walked among the patrons in the bar, carrying an unmarked collecting can. He stepped up to Timothy and shook the can gently, so that the coins chinked and clashed inside like bullets dropping into a magazine.

'For the boys,' he said with a wink and a grin. 'For the lads and the great cause. Come on now, dig into your pockets.'

Timothy looked benevolently at the small man and winked drunkenly back at him.

'Sure,' he said in his own Belfast voice, quietly, so as not to slur the words. 'Sure, am I not one of the boys myself?'

'Belfast?' The small man asked, stiffening with sudden respect. 'Are you one of the lads in Belfast then?'

'I am,' said Timothy, 'I am, but I'll say nothing more. You understand.'

He reached and gripped the small man's arm.

'Tell nobody,' he gave another drunken conspiratorial wink.

'God's blessing on you, let me shake that hand,' said the small man fervently. 'God keep you safe and strengthen your arm!'

Martin watched and heard all of this, his mouth opening once more in amazement. He was already in an alcoholic fog, and excitement pumped at his heart, catching at his breath. The small man left, and Timothy looked into his empty glass with a little smile.

'Tim,' said Martin in a hushed voice, 'Tim, are you –?'

'– I'll say nothing,' said Timothy, but smiled fondly at him. 'And you'll say nothing, either. It's the only way, Martin. The only way.'

He left next day, producing like a conjuror a bottle of perfume from his pocket for Mary. Martin he left with a crackling envelope, and a smiling warning to a wagging finger.

'Don't be opening that till I've gone now, you hear?'

He waved back through the taxi window, and was gone. Martin thought that the tenement flat seemed both empty and smaller without Timothy. Even the six crisp five-pound notes in the envelope could not fill an empty chair, and he did not hear his mother when she said with a shaking of the head: 'He's some talker, that Timothy. A great tale-spinner, he could make a living at it.'

There was a change in Martin, it seemed to Mary. He began to go regularly to mass, even to the men's club in the chapel hall on a Friday night, and Mary was pleased to see him taking his religion more seriously. That was her thought, and wrong.

Martin's interest was not religious. It was Ireland that filled his soul, not God. He listened to the Irish priest, Father O'Cahan, and revelled in the soft brogue and gentle country homilies which studded the old man's ceremony. On Friday nights in the club the talk would turn to the old days in Ireland, days that had become rosier and more entrancing as the years sped from them and they sank back into old men's tales of their youth or of their fathers' day.

Martin listened and was no longer only another unemployed youth. He knew himself to be an exiled child of Ireland, one of the wild geese in a foreign land awaiting the day of return. The older men knew that they would not return, and indeed most had no wish to leave Scotland, but Martin, in the flush of youthful discovery, began to believe that this Ireland of the past lived still, that this Ireland of the cottages and the colleens and the heroes still awaited her exiled children from across the dividing sea.

Martin kept this from his mother, another secret, and a shadow of the secrets he had shared with Timothy. So it was that when the week came which she was to spend in Leeds with her daughter, Mary had no more than the usual mother's doubts as to the wisdom of leaving her son on his own.

She was packed, ready and on the train, and looked again at Martin through the open window of the door.

'Are you sure, you'll be all right?'

'I'll be fine, Mum,' Martin hid his impatience at his mother's solicitude. 'I'm twenty next month. I'll be fine.'

'You've got enough money. Remember the paper money,' she raised her voice as the whistle blew shrill along the platform. 'Don't keep that cold pork after tomorrow.'

She leaned awkwardly through the window and Martin kissed her rouged cheek as the train began to move slowly beneath the high glass and iron roof towards the gleaming rails beyond.

'And don't get up to any mischief!' Mary called back.

'I won't, Mum,' Martin waved and stepped back as the train began to bend away from him along the curve of the rail.

'Goodbye, goodbye!' He called and waved, entirely alone for the first time in his life, already tasting the freedom and the pain.

It rained later, long and heavy, the drops sliding like translucent worms across the windows. Martin lifted his eyes above the grey tenements towards the west.

West Belfast was quiet, the storm-lashing rain driving down the stink of the last night's burnings and tear gas. The army had cleared away the fire-blackened debris of cars and lorries hijacked to barricade and burn, and the streets between the rows of terraced houses were wet and cold, with a litter of broken bricks and glass lying here and there to sign the battlegrounds.

The ink ran in blue smudges down the paper when he looked at the scribbled directions. The rain ran straight down the side of the bag and darkened his jeans where they touched.

Martin clutched his anorak tighter at the throat, and picked his way among the jagged fragments of glass beneath a gable end which proclaimed, in foot-high lettering against a background of orange, white and green: 'BRITS OUT! UP THE REPUBLIC!'

He was almost alone on the streets; only a few hurrying souls besides himself braved the torrent from the skies, but behind windows, shadows behind net curtains or in shadows aside from the direct light through the panes, Martin caught glimpses of the motionless watchers who saw him pass.

Dungarvel Street was on the other side of a sudden ugly wasteland of red ash. Martin started across the emptiness, around pools of dark-stained rainwater and past forlorn banks of struggling weeds. A patrol of eight soldiers came sharply along the terrace on the farther side, and Martin told himself that these were the oppressors of his countrymen, but strangely, the words would not take in his mind, and all he really felt was something like disbelief at the sight of these silent running men, dressed in drab green and brown combat gear, and holding ungainly black rifles across their chests. The last two soldiers watched only to the rear, doubling back behind each other to drop and crouch in doorways. As Martin crossed into Dungarvel Street he looked at their white, dirt-streaked faces and saw, with a quickening of disbelief, that a black and dripping rifle muzzle pointed straight at him, and followed his footsteps until the corner took him from its sights.

Martin walked briskly down the street, the tremors in his stomach subsiding, but now even more eager to get indoors and out of the rain. He knocked on Timothy's door. No answer. He knocked again, harder. Again no answer, and with mounting frustration, realizing that Timothy must be out working, he stepped back from the door, glancing up and down the street, turning his head so that the eager rain found its way down inside his collar. From the edge of his vision he saw a corner of the curtain twitch in the neighbour window.

He knocked on that door, twice, before he heard a reluctant voice, an old woman's voice from deep within the hallway.

'Who's that?' The words were quiet as if whispered in the hope that they would not be heard.

'I'm Timothy Maguire's nephew, Martin. He's not in the house, do you know where he'll be?'

'His nephew, do you say?' Frail and suspicious words.

'Yes! Do you know where he is?'

'You might be a nephew, but you're not from here.'

'I'm from Glasgow!' Martin almost shouted with frustration. 'His sister's son, Martin O'Brien!'

'Glasgow.' The old voice hesitated, and relented only a little. 'He'll be working. He's never home before five.'

Martin turned back into the rain and retraced his steps down the street and across the empty waste to a pub he had passed on a corner. Screens of thick wire mesh stretched across the windows like stiff grey nets, with crisp bags and scraps of dirty newspaper caught between the wire and the unwashed glass. The door was narrow and heavy, pitted and scarred like a target.

Inside, the pub was dark, dark and silent, the dim afternoon's light seeping weakly through the windows, and the half-dozen men staring wordlessly at Martin. He pushed back the hood of his anorak, and the rain rolled down his shoulders to the floor, emphasizing the silence with the pattering of the drops breaking upon the floor. The barman raised his eyebrows interrogatively as Martin stepped up to the bar.

'Pint of heavy, please,' Martin put his bag on the floor,

and when there were no words in response, he added, 'Terrible wet today.'

'It is,' the barman passed him the full pint glass and held out his hand.

Martin paid, and drank, turning to lean on the bartop. He could see the other men watching him, and he tried a friendly smile and a nod, and the men looked unsmilingly back at him, and then stirred. One, balding and middle-aged in a donkey jacket, walked around Martin and stood at his elbow, between him and the door. Another, younger, perhaps in his late twenties, stroked back his wet black hair and came to lean on the bar in front of Martin, looking him up and down with a thoughtful pursing of his mouth. Martin caught his dark eyes for an instant, and felt uneasy as those eyes slid away across his face and down his length, finally studying the bag at his feet. The young man lifted his head, and looked steadily at Martin.

'Come far?' He had a soft, almost sleepy voice.

'From Glasgow,' Martin replied, then quickly, 'to see my uncle, Timothy Maguire, Dungarvel Street.'

'I thought I recognized the accent. You'll be Scottish, then?'

'I'm Irish by blood. O'Brien. Timothy's my mother's brother.'

'Common enough names, O'Brien and Maguire. But you sound Scottish to me.'

Martin thought he heard a hard edge pushing into the soft voice; a hard edge, a hint of menace, turning towards threat. He could almost feel the man behind staring at him. He began to feel afraid, and swallowed a gulp of beer to steal seconds in which to mask his fear.

'Born and brought up in Glasgow, I suppose I do,' he said at last, and was glad to hear his voice did not tremble.

He lifted his glass and began to drink hastily, to finish and leave. The young man put a hand on his arm.

'Take your time,' he said easily. 'Aren't we just having a wee talk?'

'I'm off to see my uncle.' Martin put down his glass.

'Timothy Maguire? Well, what's a name after all? And this place is thick with the Maguires.'

'What do you mean?' demanded Martin, talking braver than he felt.

'You could pick any name from a phone book, could you not?'

'Look,' Martin bent to pick up his bag. 'I'm over to see my uncle, and I'm going now.'

'You're not,' and the young man gave a slight nod.

The balding man gripped Martin by the arms, and the young man casually gripped his right wrist and turned it outwards, so that his fingers loosened on the handle, and let the bag fall. Martin cursed and struggled, and the balding man slammed him hard against the bar, twice, winding him. He gasped for breath, blinking back tears of pain, and watched his belongings being impatiently scattered on to the bartop. Finally, the young man held the bag upside down and shook it, then let it fall to the floor.

'Nothing,' he said, and looked at Martin. 'Not a thing. Maybe it's the truth.'

'Take no chances, Michael,' said the balding man.

'Do I ever?' asked the young man irritably, and turned to the other men. 'Patrick, keep a look-out. Sean, find this Timothy Maguire, and bring him.'

The men left. Michael studied Martin again and jerked his head towards a corner with a small rickety table and two chairs.

'Put him over there, Peter. Back towards the door.'

Martin was pushed down sharply into the chair. His ribs ached and he touched them gingerly. He was afraid now, thoroughly afraid.

'What's going on?' he asked, speaking in short gasps, catching at his breath. 'What do you want with me?'

'Indeed,' said Michael, and sat opposite him, 'and that's the whole point – what's going on. This is Ireland. There's a war going on, and you fit the wrong way for us to be happy about you strolling in here and chatting about the weather.'

The barman stuffed Martin's clothes back into the bag, and set it on the bartop.

Michael ticked off his fingers in a casual, unexcited manner, like a teacher making something very plain.

'You're Scottish. You've short hair. You're what – twenty, nineteen?'

'Nineteen,' Martin's mouth trembled and he quickly wiped his hand across it to cover his fear.

'Well, all that means one thing only to me.' Michael leaned forward as if to confide. 'Spy. Soldier. Spy.'

'My name's O'Brien! I'm a Catholic!'

'There's plenty Scottish soldiers with Irish names go to mass. And I don't even know your name is O'Brien, now do I?'

'My uncle will tell you!' Martin said quickly. 'Christ, he's one of the lads himself!'

'One of the lads?' mused Michael. 'A brave freedom fighter is he? Well, well.'

The balding man put a hand on Martin's shoulder and squeezed hard, digging his fingers into the sinews behind the collar bone.

'Do we interrogate him?' he said to Michael.

'You're that eager, Peter,' Michael sighed and sat back in

the squeaking wooden chair. 'He could be telling us the truth. Well, part of the truth.'

'In which case we'll know,' said the balding man, 'and there could still be time for the other business.'

He took out a cigarette and lit it, drew deeply and then took the cigarette from his mouth and blew on the coal so that it burned redly. He looked at Michael.

'I don't think so,' said Michael. 'Use it to give yourself cancer instead.'

Peter laughed and drew in a breath of smoke. After a little while he gripped Martin's shoulder once more, and dug his fingers even harder, searching for the pain centres. Martin stood it for a short while, then the hard fingers sent an agonizing spasm through his shoulder and arm. He twisted away and reached up to massage his shoulder.

'Did that hurt?' asked Peter.

'Yes.' Martin felt hatred coming behind the fear.

'Well that's a little indication,' said Peter. 'If you're not what you say you are, that pain will be like a nothing.'

'Leave him alone,' said Michael sharply. 'Violence is a tool, not a pleasure.'

'God, Michael,' Peter grinned maliciously. 'Aren't you becoming the intellectual?'

'You shut up,' said Michael. 'Do you hear me? Shut up!'

Martin listened, and the Ireland of the tales suffocated and died inside him.

Timothy came at last, dressed in his overalls, his face pale and sweating and trying to smile. Michael looked him up and down thoughtfully, as he had earlier inspected Martin.

'Well,' he said finally. 'I know you, Maguire, and you know me. You're no danger to us, or to the enemy. Who's this boy?'

'My nephew, Martin.' Timothy was subdued.

'I'm not sure, Maguire, and I don't take chances. He looks like one of those bloody-minded Scots soldiers to me.'

'He's only a boy!' Timothy took a pace forward.

'I've got boys of his age dying out there,' said Michael evenly, 'and so have the Brits.'

He stood up and walked to stand only a foot away from Timothy, looking levelly into his eyes. Martin saw Timothy turn even paler and look away, down at the floor, shuffling his feet a little.

'Your nephew is under the impression, Maguire, that you're a bold Fenian man, a freedom fighter, one of the lads.'

'Him?' Peter laughed. 'The most he could fight would be a full glass.'

'No, no, a mistake!' Timothy licked his lips. 'I've the greatest respect for you, and I pay my contributions with the best, but I'd never claim your glory for myself! No, never!'

'I should hope you would not,' said Michael, and his eyes did not move from Timothy's face. 'I'm fighting a revolutionary war, and there's enough trouble for us all, without the need to enforce discipline on such as you.'

He put a hand into his jacket pocket, and brought out a blue steel revolver. Timothy stiffened, licking his lips again. Martin could almost feel his fear; almost smell his terror. Michael tapped Timothy on the elbow with the revolver barrel.

'You take my meaning?' he asked, and put the gun back in his pocket.

Timothy nodded, making small stuttering noises, blinking rapidly.

'Like I said,' Michael continued, 'I'm fighting a revolutionary war, and you've never even thrown a bloody brick, let alone been on active service!'

'My father died for Ireland!' said Timothy hoarsely.

'Sure,' said Michael with contempt. 'Is that not your style? Another man's deeds again!'

'I'll make it up to you for your trouble, I will!'

'Oh, you will,' agreed Michael. 'You'll be hearing from us. Now, get out, the pair of you.'

Martin stood up, and Peter tossed his bag at him, hard, using both hands, as if throwing a medicine ball.

'You're a lucky boy. Michael's getting soft!'

'Enough of that!' Michael rounded on him. 'Save your criticisms for the proper time, not here!'

He turned back to Timothy and Martin, still standing without moving.

'I said, get out!' And he turned to the bar and unbidden the barman placed a pint in his hand.

Timothy and Martin walked awkwardly down the street, silence between them. The rain had stopped, and grey clouds swept overhead like tattered banners.

'Come on, we'll go up to the house,' said Timothy at last.

'No,' said Martin. 'I don't want to stay, not after that.'

'They won't trouble you again, Martin,' Timothy spread his hands, 'don't judge us by that!'

'Us?' Martin sneered, and stopped walking, to look at his uncle. 'Us? What's this "us"? You've never thrown a brick, remember?'

A car drove past with the slow speed of a hearse, the passenger gazing out the side window at them. Martin wondered what work they were engaged upon.

'If I'd known you were coming!' Timothy pleaded. 'Martin, you must see, you just got in the way.'

'Do you never wonder who else "just got in the way"? Is that how the cause is won?'

'Martin, Martin! You're upset, and I don't blame you.

Come on up to the house, at least for the night, and I'll drive
you to Larne tomorrow.'

'No, I'm going,' Martin looked up and down the street for
the way out of the terraces and back to the railway station.

'Martin, please. Don't let us part like this.'

Martin looked stiffly past, and Timothy sighed and
looked down at his shoes and the wet pavement. There was
silver creeping into his hair, and a thinning begun at the
crown of his head. Martin felt a new emotion: pity.

'Well, just for tonight, then,' he said, and saw Timothy lift
his head and smile a growing shadow of his old beaming
smile.

That evening, while Timothy cooked, whistling with his
jauntiness mostly restored by a large whiskey, Martin
looked out the window at the huddled row of terraced
houses opposite, on the other side of the twilight street. A
puddle caught the light from the window in a lonely splash
of illumination, and he thought with longing of tall grey
tenements in the rain.

After the War

DOUGLAS DUNN

The soldiers came, brewed tea in Snoddy's field
Beside the wood from where we watched them pee
In Snoddy's stagnant pond, small boys hidden
In pines and firs. The soldiers stood or sat
Ten minutes in the field, some officers apart
With the select problems of a map. Before,
Soldiers were imagined, we were them, gunfire
In our mouths, most cunning local skirmishers.
Their sudden arrival silenced us. I lay down
On the grass and saw the blue shards of an egg
We'd broken, its warm yolk on the green grass,
And pine cones like little hand grenades.

One burst from an imaginary Browning,
A grenade well thrown by a child's arm,
And all these faces like our fathers' faces
Would fall back bleeding, trucks would burst in flames,
A blood-stained map would float on Snoddy's pond.
Our ambush made the soldiers laugh, and some
Made booming noises from behind real rifles
As we ran among them begging for badges,
Our plimsolls on the fallen May-blossom
Like boots on the faces of dead children.
But one of us had left. I saw him go
Out through the gate, I heard him on the road

Running to his mother's house. They lived alone,
Behind a hedge round an untended garden
Filled with broken toys, abrasive loss;
A swing that creaked, a rusted bicycle.
He went inside just as the convoy passed.

Oor Hamlet

ADAM MCNAUGHTAN

There was this king sleeping in his gairden a' alane
When his brither in his ear drapped a wee tait o' henbane.
Then he stole his brither's crown and his money and his
    widow
But the deid king walked and goat his son and said, 'Heh,
    listen, kiddo!'
'Ah've been killt and it's your duty to take revenge oan
    Claudius.
Kill him quick and clean and show the nation whit a fraud
    he is.'
The boay says, 'Right, Ah'll dae it, but Ah'll huvti play it
    crafty.
So that naeb'dy will suspect me, Ah'll kid oan that Ah'm a
    daftie.'

So wi' a' except Horatio (and he trusts him as a friend),
Hamlet – that's the boay – kids oan he's roon the bend,
And because he wisnae ready for obligatory killing
He tried to make the king think he was tuppence aff the
    shilling;
Took the mickey oot Polonius, treatit poor Ophelia vile,
And tellt Rosencrantz and Guildenstern that Denmark was
    a jile.
Then a troupe o' travelling actors, like 7.84
Arrived to dae a special wan-night gig in Elsinore.

Hamlet, Hamlet! Loved his mammy.
Hamlet, Hamlet! Acting balmy.
Hamlet, Hamlet! Hesitating.
Wonders if the ghost's a cheat and that is why he's
waiting.

Then Hamlet wrote a scene for the players to enact,
While Horatio and him would watch to see if Claudius
cracked.
The play was ca'd 'The Mousetrap', (No the wan that's
running noo)
And sure enough, the king walked oot afore the scene was
through.
So Hamlet's goat the proof that Claudius gied his da the
dose,
The only problem being noo that Claudius knows he
knows.
So while Hamlet tells his ma that her new husband's no a
fit wan,
Uncle Claud pits oot a contract wi' the English King as
hit-man.

And when Hamlet killed Polonius, the concealed corpus
delecti
Was the king's excuse to send him for an English hempen
necktie,
Wi' Rosencrantz and Guildenstern to make sure he goat
there,
But Hamlet jumped the boat and pit the finger oan that
pair.
Meanwhile, Laertes heard his da had been stabbed through
the arras;

He came racing back to Elsinore toute-suite, hot-foot fae
    Paris.
And Ophelia, wi' her da killt by the man she wished to
    marry –
Efter saying it wi' flooers, she committit hari-kari.

    Hamlet, Hamlet! Nae messin!
    Hamlet, Hamlet! Learnt his lesson.
    Hamlet, Hamlet! Yorick's crust
    Convinced him that men, good or bad, at last must
      come to dust.

Then Laertes loast the place and was demanding
    retribution,
But the king said, 'Keep the heid and Ah'll provide ye a
    solution.'
And he arranged a sword-fight wi' the interestit perties,
Wi' a bluntit sword for Hamlet and a shairp sword for
    Laertes.
And to make things double-sure – the auld belt and braces
    line –
He fixed a poisont sword-tip and a poisont cup o' wine,
And the poisont sword goat Hamlet but Laertes went and
    muffed it,
'Cause he goat stabbed hissel and he confessed afore he
    snuffed it.

Then Hamlet's mammy drank the wine and as her face
    turnt blue,
Hamlet says, 'Ah quite believe the king's a baddy noo.'
'Incestuous, murd'rous, damned Dane,' he said, to be
    precise,
And made up for hesitating by killing Claudius twice;

'Cause he stabbed him wi' the sword and forced the wine
    atween his lips
Then he said, 'The rest is silence.' That was Hamlet hud his
    chips.
They fired a volley ower him that shook the topmost rafter
And Fortinbras, knee-deep in Danes, lived happy ever
    after.

    Hamlet, Hamlet! Aw the gory!
    Hamlet, Hamlet! End of story.
    Hamlet, Hamlet! Ah'm away!
    If you think this is boring, you should read the bloody
        play!

The Great McGunnigle

EDWARD BOYLE

It was the start of a new term at St Andrew's High School in Wellshaw, the grey Lanarkshire steel manufacturing town. As his parents were still on holiday and no gentle mother's hand to stir him in the morning, young Milloy had set the radio alarm for 7.45. He awoke with the voice of Terry Wogan announcing an old number by the Seekers, 'The Carnival Is Over', and indeed for Alex, the carnival was over, the holidays were over, seven weeks of bliss were about to give way to many months of worry. Eyelids still heavy, his first conscious thought was of school and the dawning realization that he might again have that big swine, McGunnigle, for English.

'Surely,' he thought, 'I'll not have McGunnigle this year.' Milloy was starting his fifth term at school and in his previous year had the ultimate misfortune to meet up with McGunnigle, the bane of his life. In his first, second and third years he had been lucky enough not to have drawn the great big toerag, for there were 1,100 pupils and fourteen teachers in the English department. In fourth year with the odds the same, he and McGunnigle had met up and for the first time Milloy hated school, all because of that one hulking brute, all five feet eleven of him. Now the odds had shortened and with only 380 pupils taking Higher English, the chances of getting McGunnigle again were all the more likely. But perhaps the fates would be kinder this time.

Several times the previous year, Milloy had felt like packing it up. On one occasion, after a last period altercation with McGunnigle, he had come home in so obviously distraught a state that his mother had asked what was wrong. Ordinarily, Milloy did not tell of what went on in school unless it was something unconnected with the classroom like a parents' meeting or a school function such as a PT dance or a Fayre. This time he had almost burst into tears and at his mother's insistence, told of his misery. She had been aghast but felt that there was little she could do to help her son. She recalled earlier occasions when Alex was subjected to bullying at his primary school, that interviewing headmistress and staff had helped little. In truth, she like many parents, felt out of her depth visiting a school, whether the corridors were bustling at breaks or quiet during classes. Neither mother nor son would confide in father, a security van driver, who was able to look after himself and thought his son should be capable of doing the same.

Strangely enough the worst confrontations between pupil and teacher had not been in class but at several school functions. Milloy had brought to a Hallowe'en party a girlfriend who had to suffer close attention from McGunnigle racing across the floor to grab Greta several times and get her to dance with him, Milloy looking on in silent rage. At the tea interval Greta whispered to her partner that she could smell drink off McGunnigle and that when they were dancing he ran his fingers down the length of her spine. When next McGunnigle made an approach, Milloy intervened, there was a short flurry, not enough to attract general attention, thanks to the nearby presence of two teachers who separated the would-be adversaries. On the way home when Greta aired her grievances, Milloy ground his teeth and silently swore that one day he would flatten McGunnigle, no matter the consequences.

Another vexation was when Mrs Milloy was helping with the 'White Elephant' stall at the annual school fête. During its two hours duration, McGunnigle had hardly quit the vicinity, staring at Mrs Milloy, minutes at a time, and offering derisory sums of money for displayed items. Nearing the end of the sale he had put down ten pence for an indoor TV aerial and wanted to take a small dainty hedgehog pincushion for five pence. 'Sure no one will come and buy that now,' he leered, 'the sale's nearly over!' Mrs Milloy ignored him and bought the pincushion for the asking price of one pound.

Further wranglings occurred in class, mainly accusations over homework, copying in exams, inattention and dumb insolence.

'You did this homework in the bog by the look of it.'

'You copied chunks of this essay out of the *Reader's Digest*.'

'How come you and Wilson here have the same answers?'

Almost every day Milloy could expect trouble from McGunnigle and almost every day Milloy felt like walking out of school. During that summer vacation, his mother had tried to comfort him. 'Perhaps you won't get him in fifth year. Remember that this is a short term for fifth year, the Highers begin at the end of April and you won't see him when the exams are over. Try to be patient for you don't want to do anything foolish at this stage and ruin your career.' Milloy listened to her but was not comforted. An inner voice told him that he would be fated to meet up with McGunnigle this term and short one or not, it would be hell.

It was all so unfair; he was but five feet eight in height, weighed eight stone eleven pounds and had never been all that strong and active; his only claim to athletic prowess had been at primary school when the football team had been short of a player, the teacher had picked him blindly from among the few pupils who turned up to watch the match; he was quite fast and played as a nippy winger avoiding physical contact as far as possible. McGunnigle was nearly six feet tall, scaled ten stone ten pounds and was active in school sports; Milloy watched him enviously in the gym, climbing ropes, somersaulting over the horse and playing basketball at which with his height he was easily the leading goal snatcher. In the annual Teachers v Pupils soccer game, McGunnigle and Milloy were both playing with Milloy coming off worse; his opponent was playing 'sweeper' and had twice swept Milloy on to the surrounding cinder track thereby sustaining an annoying gravel rash on both knees. These his mother had tenderly bathed and bound, again saying nothing to her husband.

That sunny August morn he rolled reluctantly out of bed to face the oncoming day. He made breakfast from the cornflakes and eggs that his mother had provided, lunch he could get at school and evening dinner at his aunt's down the road. It was an easy ten minutes walk to school, a journey however he did not enjoy for he was apt to meet McGunnigle who lived in the same area and would cross the road or bring his brisk walk to a dawdle if he saw his tormentor in the distance. There would however be no chance of an encounter that particular day as pupils and teachers did not meet one another until ten o'clock on opening day.

Later with pounding heart he saw the timetables and class lists. To his horror but not to his surprise, he had McGunnigle for English. The only consolation and small consolation at that was the class met for four double and one single period per week and this was not one of the days. All he could hope for now was that something drastic would happen to McGunnigle; perhaps his father, an electrical engineer, would emigrate to Australia or South Africa in response to one of those alluring newspaper advertisements; perhaps he would break a leg, or better still, his neck, when doing one of his handsprings in the gym; or perhaps . . .

But that term was to run its fateful course. With the first meeting of the class, Milloy could feel the old tension as though there had been no intervening holidays and he could sense McGunnigle's sardonic gaze upon him even when the class was busy working. The class was well aware of the situation and waited, part in hope, part in trepidation, for the outbreak of hostilities. But open war did not occur immediately, probably because there is a feeling of freshness and light at the start of a new term; the building is clean and smelling of fragrant disinfectant, the floors are gleaming, the walls scrubbed free of graffiti, shining blackboards and desks inviting renewed effort, the windows repaired and all intact. Unfortunately as the freshness evaporates the old animosities reappear, and so was it with Milloy and McGunnigle.

Three weeks and twenty-seven periods later the inevitable occurred and it sprang from the old source, accusation of slovenly work at home and class, copying, inattention and insolence. Fundamentally Milloy was peace loving and exercised great patience in face of provocation, trying to go about his work ignoring the other's presence, keeping as it were to his own side of the arena. It was actually homework that caused the final break.

'I don't remember getting your last homework.'

'What homework was that?'

'The appreciation of Cowper.'

'Y'mean Davie Cooper? Y'could hardly expect me to write an appreciation of a Rangers player.'

'Don't be smart.'

'Oh, I'm not Smart, he's in 5C.'

That was it. Milloy could take no more and all restraint vanished. But he was conscious of his disadvantage in height and weight and knew that if he went in with bare fists, he would never get within arm's length of the swine. Instinctively he remembered a weapon close at hand, the board ruler. It lay conveniently projecting over the teacher's desk, five feet long, six inches broad, solid oak with sharp edge. He grabbed, advanced a few feet between desks, crashed it down on his adversary's head and when he put up his hands for protection, brought the ruler in a full force arc on his fingers. McGunnigle screamed; Milloy shivered in elation. In utter silence the class stared with unbelieving eyes and only after a few seconds broke into a babble of sighs, jeers and cheers, just as dismissal bell rang.

Milloy dropped his weapon and stumbled from the room, a thin smile of satisfaction on his face.

'That's it,' he thought to himself, 'that's it at last and I don't give a damn if that's the last of me and St Andrew's. It was worth it, bloody well worth it.'

He was in the toilet splashing his face with water when Hoban, the Deputy Rector, touched his shoulder.

'The Head wants to see you in his room.'

Milloy nodded and dried his hands and face with a paper towel. Curious eyes, some friendly, some hostile, watched his progress on the two minute walk across the school to the Head's study. Milloy, still flushed, knocked timidly and the green light above the door blinked, bidding him enter. The Rector who was looking out the window turned grim-faced to confront Milloy.

'Well . . . this is a serious business and I don't see what I can do to help you. I can't keep it within the school. Assaulting a pupil is a police matter, Mr Milloy.'

Two Birds

LIZ LOCHHEAD

on each of these two
cards from you blue-
tacked to the wall above
my writing table.

on
torn-edge Japanese hand-
made wood-paper flecked
with gold
two
bigwinged blacktipped wild
geese are caught in perfect
midflight assymetry on the blue
getting there.
and yet there's effort in it too,

the master artist does not deny it
— as on this cracked valentine
we found at the market stall, all
lovey-dovey these two
conventional circa
nineteen-ten bluebirds, one with
flower, one with billet-doux
above linked hands entwined
through hearts, a pretty
ditty about Constancy

that made us smile.
hearts are not
pretty frames for anything, all
rococo forget-me-nots of cloying
Edwardiana.
they're raw and red
they jump, we know they do.

I say still: birds can be airmail blue
and hearts can be true.

A Picture of Zoe

LIAM STEWART

I've got a picture of Zoe. I've still kept it after a year. It's a drawing by the Artist, and there he is now, near where I'm sitting, still sketching away trying to make a living.

The old lady approved of Zoe the first minute she saw her. It was the look of her for a start, all bright and clean on the grimy street, with the blonde hair bouncing about like a shampoo advert. I could see that look in the old lady's eyes when she met us going to her work that day. They're roaming over the details, impressed, storing them up for later reference: the spotless creamy coat, the shiny mauve high heels (not too high), the matching shoulder-bag and the black skirt made of that good quality material. And when Zoe opened her mouth, that was it! The old lady's over the moon! Zoe's well-spoken. The Bearsden accent set the seal on what the old lady saw as a very nice little package.

The old lady herself has always had this thing about talking properly: saying 'you' instead of 'yous', things like that. She's not that good at it herself, but she admires folk that can do it. It's all because she thinks she's a cut above this area. She even wears chiffon scarves and puts on red nail polish to go out to her cleaning job. Glamour girl at 48. It's a bit pathetic, if you could see it.

When I got back home to the scheme that night, she's sitting by the fire in her dressing-gown, drinking coffee and puffing a fag, still smirking to herself even though it's a sad picture on the telly.

'My! That's a nice girl, son!' she says, taking a sip of her coffee and winking at me. 'Where did you meet her?'

She knew it must have been somewhere good. Not the bus queue or the social security or the chippie or anywhere in this dump, with the boarded-up houses and the packs of scabby dogs marauding through the closes and over the waste ground. Oh no! She could see at a glance Zoe had never picked her way through this terrain.

Zoe was a college girl. Dunky had this girlfriend that was training to be a teacher, and Zoe was her pal. So one night Zoe and me met up along with Dunky and the girlfriend. That was how it all started, a sort of blind date. I was told afterwards that she thought I was a nice-looking boy. Actually, she wasn't the first to hold this opinion and, I have to admit, apart from everything else about her, she had her curves in the right places. So the old animal attraction was there all right. But it struck me pretty soon that, for some-body who was going to be a teacher, Zoe knew less about the real world than the old lady's budgie. Everything was 'gorgeous' (with the head cocked on one side) or 'awful' (with the eyes aghast).

For me, it was a bit of a laugh at first going out with somebody who talked like Zoe. To the mates, when they found out about it, it was me going out with a pure snob. I often wondered what Zoe was thinking about those first few times we went out. It was hard to know. If I looked at her quickly, before she had time to flick on the old smile, and caught her in one of those quizzical glances she thought I didn't notice, it looked as though she regarded me as from another species, one of the lower orders who might give her some useful material for one of her school projects.

And God! Was she out of touch! I don't know where she usually went, but sometimes when I was out with her she seemed to be looking about herself as if she thought there was Apaches up every close. And her mouth was pursed so tight you would have thought there was something putrid in the atmosphere.

That's the way it looked that first time at The Happy Moon Chinese restaurant in the Dumbarton Road. I thought I better play a strong card as an opener – a good night out, a good meal. I had been to this particular grub shop before, with Dunky and Tam, and it had not been too bad at all.

Well, as soon as I step over the threshold with Zoe I can see it isn't such a high-class establishment as it seemed the last time. After drifting along the street breathing in Zoe's perfume, the smell of stale fat is too noticeable. Zoe's eyes are darting about as if I've brought her to an opium den in Hong Kong, and though she makes a big effort to keep nattering and flashing the old teeth, I can see she's ill at ease in such shabby surroundings. She takes in the shortcomings of the place and so do I: the carpet worn in patches through to the backing, the yellow stains like big suns on the table-cloth and, next to the kitchen door on the green flock wallpaper, a big mark that looks like a blotch of blood or where somebody has flung a plate of something they weren't satisfied with. It's dimly lit right enough, but the only other customers are an old couple who look like a pair of dossers and keep staring over at us out of their shadowy corner.

But it was what happened when we were in the middle of our dinner (quite a nice wee chicken chow mein that I think she was even beginning to enjoy) that really put the tin-lid on it. This drunk guy staggers in, unnoticed as it happens, and sinks down at the table next to us. I can see Zoe stiffening and leaning away from him. The guy's head's rolling about, but somehow or other he manages to convey his order, and a minute later a bowl of chicken noodle soup (the burn-the-mouth kind we've just had) is plunked down in front of him, with the flowery china spoon. But by this time he has begun to nod off to sleep. His arms have slipped down over the sides of his chair and his head is sagging down towards his chicken noodle. Down he goes till his nose makes contact with the soup. It scalds him enough to jerk him a foot up and almost open his heavy lids. Then he droops down again, the nose dips into the chicken noodle and he jerks up again. And so it goes on, like one of those pecking toys or as if there's a spring in his spine. By this time he has an audience. It's an entertainment to the old pair chomping away in their corner, and the waiter and manager are standing watching, arms folded, jabbering away in Chinese. The upward jerks are reduced to about four inches now, whether because the guy's sinking into a deeper sleep or his nose is getting acclimatized, I don't know. But the Chinese boys obviously see a danger that the soup might get spilled or our pecking friend might get drowned, so the manager strides over and whips the bowl out from under the guy's nose. He shakes him for about twenty seconds and then shoves a bill into his hand, jabbering away the whole time. Obviously he's telling him to cough up for the soup and then get out. The guy slumps back in his chair, holding the bill out at arm's length, trying to read it through his drunken stupor.

In his state it might as well be in Cantonese, but vaguely the aggro of the situation begins to dawn on him and he goes into a Clint Eastwood act. He crumples the bill and drops it on the floor, trying to stare at The Happy Moon boys the whole time. Then he points his finger at the manager.

'You're at it,' he says slowly, . . . 'I've been oot in India.'

There's no answer to that. You have to laugh. But, Christ, the manager dives straight into the argument and the waiter backs him up. This is not India, they're shouting, and quoting him the price of chickens and the upkeep of The Happy Moon and asking him when he was in India anyway.

However, the chicken noodle guy then decides to be magnanimous. He holds up his hand, dismissing the argument, and heaves himself on to his feet, just about cowping the table in the process. He's standing there rocking about as if he's on a ship, digging deep into the pockets of his baggy blue suit. They're scrabbling about picking up sauce bottles and straightening the table.

'Right, now,' he asks contemptuously, counting the pile of change he's dug out, 'how much is your soup?'

But it transpires he hasn't got enough, so they waive the bill and start huckling him out the door. This could have been a very bad move because the guy breaks free and starts to swear at them. But at the last minute they have the sense to hold back and let him do a dusting-off routine and tell them, as he stumbles out the door, that he'll never eat in The Happy Moon again and neither will his friends and he'll ruin them. They're clearing his table when the door swings open again and he steps back in. I knew it.

'Your soup was shitey, anyhow!' he says, gives them the V-sign and falls back through the door.

It's a riveting scene. I keep my eyes on the door for a couple of seconds to see if he'll do another encore, and then I look at Zoe. Her eyes are wide.

'How awful!' she says. 'That poor man looked as though he could have done with a bowl of soup.'

Poor man! A bowl of soup! Christ! The guy looked as if he'd been pouring booze down his throat the whole day. But I can see an expression on Zoe's face that tells me she really thinks it was a distasteful incident. So, at the bus stop, I say to her that I am sorry that her evening had been spoiled.

'Oh don't be silly, Gerry!' she says, giving me a peck on the cheek. 'Really! It was a lovely meal,' and she flashes the smile, maybe just a bit less bright than usual.

That was Zoe – Queen of the Bearsden soup-kitchen. But the trouble was, and Glasgow being what it is, when she was out with me she came much closer to the unwashed orders than any meals-on-wheels Bearsden lady might ever have desired. No car you see. It had to be buses and walking in the city streets, and going to much lower-class places than it seemed she was used to.

So the next time we ventured out for something to eat, I decided to take her somewhere in the centre of the town. As usual, she says she's easy where we go, so I suggest The South Pacific. It's quite a good eating shop, a cut above the usual Wimpy Bar type places and it's licensed. It's self-service right enough, but the haddock and chips is always good and they give you a big helping. Everything's going very smoothly in fact, until we come into contact with the Artist. This is an old guy who always carries a drawing-pad about with him and a row of pencils in the top pocket of his jacket. He gives you that impression somehow of a boy who gambled at one time, but never quite made it. He's always unshaven and he wears a soft, brown hat with greasy stains on the brim. There's one or two places in the town where he's allowed to come into your company and ask if you want a charcoal sketch of yourself for a pound. The South Pacific is one of these places. Now, I had seen him doing his routine before, but, of course, had always given him the knock-back myself, never having had a pound to spare. But anyway, he's there that day and he homes in on me and Zoe and, of course, it's Zoe he wants to sketch. So she gives him the smile and we say go ahead.

He's rabbiting away the whole time as he does the sketch with what looks like an ordinary school pencil with the Green Cross Code on it. Then he comes with the line, 'Now what colour are your eyes, my dear?', looking into Zoe's eyes. 'Ah yes, a lovely blue,' he says, taking out his blue pencil and colouring in the eyes. He does the same with his red one for the lips. Seeing it upside down, I'm not impressed, and when he hands it over I can see, and I'm no art critic, that it's a joke – something maybe a kid of seven would do. He's just drawn an oval in a hard line, added basic eye, nose and mouth shapes, scribbled on a few squiggles for the hair and then coloured in the eyes and lips, and that's it. It's humanoid. It could be anybody.

'Do you not see yourself like that, dear? Well, there you are. That's the way the Artist sees you.'

His patter's terrible. I feel like telling him to get lost, but Zoe might think I'm too tight to pay the pound so I give him it. Zoe smiles and thanks him. The Artist tips his greasy hat and slides out the seat to look for some other sucker. I turn and see Zoe looking down her nose at the paper in her hand, as if she thinks it's an insult.

'It's not really very good,' I say casually, 'you don't have to keep it.'

'Oh no! It's lovely, Gerry! Really! Honest! It was really sweet of you to pay for it.' She puts it away carefully in her bag.

And that's the way it went on. Whenever Zoe and me walked through the town, we seemed to draw these people like magnets: the tramps and the winos and the hard-luck merchants. Zoe would rummage in the mauve handbag and out would come the purse and she would flash the old smile and give them the hand-out, like one of those ladies in the old days giving alms to the needy. It was a bit embarrassing to tell you the truth. However, we still went out together. There was still the animal attraction as I said, though mind you things were going a bit slow in that direction and I wasn't sure why. One thing that was always on my mind was that she had never invited me out to the Bearsden homestead, which I thought might have been a better bet than the scheme with the old lady sitting smoking at the fire.

One night after we had been going out for about two months, I had a dream about Zoe – one of those erotic dreams. It was nice at first. You know the kind. The two of us splashing about naked underneath a waterfall in a beauti-ful sunny hollow – Walt Disney for adults. Then we're getting dressed and I overhear her saying on the phone (this is back in the beach-house or the log cabin or somewhere), 'I can't speak now, Nigel. I'm still with the tramp.' I'm blazing mad and just about to confront her ... and that's all I remember of the dream.

A dream always makes you think. It gives you a strange feeling. I'm sitting toasting my toes by the fire and sipping my coffee. It's waterfalls outside and I don't want to go. I just want to sit here and try to think about the dream and see how it feels.

'Remember you've got to sign on,' the old lady says from the other side of the fire, waking me out of my day-dream. 'Are you still going out with that nice girl, son?' she asks, taking a big drag on her fag. 'When are you going to bring her home for her tea?'

She's winking again. I mutter something and scuttle through to the bedroom to get dressed. Bring her here? Oh no! I've had enough of Zoe's hollow smiles at me and my patch. Bringing her home to the old lady's fawning patter just would not do. No way. I can imagine the old lady curtseying or something and skelping the chair with a duster before Zoe put her bum on it.

What with that dream that wouldn't stop going round in my head, and the grey rain drizzling down all day and something funny in Zoe's voice on the phone last night, I wasn't looking forward to seeing her that night. I was to meet her outside the Odeon at eight, so I decided to have a couple of drinks first – just to get out of the rain and stay away from the old lady.

I drift into Lauder's in Sauchiehall Street at about six. As usual it's mobbed, vibrating with the juke-box. There's nobody I know so it's pleasant enough to stand at the bar, letting the bitter taste of a pint of Guinness soothe my worries, relaxing in the anonymity of the crowd. It engulfs you – the noise, the colours, the smell of the drink and the perfume. I get another pint of Guinness and find a corner to sit and read my paper. We're getting Jim Reeves from the old juke-box now – 'You're the only good thing'.

The customary perusal of the Situations Vacant: sales reps mostly. 'Do you want to make 25,000 a year? You can if you're the right sort of bloke.'

I know I'm the wrong sort, so I fold the paper over to the crossword. This is one big aspect of the problem, of course, me being unemployed and going out with Zoe, the doctor's daughter. I'm sure it's got a lot to do with me not getting anywhere near Bearsden. Can you imagine me sitting in the Bearsden lounge, sipping the Martini, when the old boy strolls in from the golf-course. 'Well Zoe, so this is the young man who's been entertaining you these last few weeks. Pleased to meet you, my boy. What profession are you hoping to enter yourself?'

I'm not making much of the crossword, so I sink another

pint and throw a whisky down after it. Well, there you are. What's green and gets you drunk? Chartreuse? Crème de Menthe? No, a giro. Actually, the drink's beginning to warm me up a bit. That funny feeling from the dream is beginning to die away. I'm getting it straight in my mind what I want to say to Zoe. I'm finally going to tell her straight. I'm not getting aggressive. I don't get aggressive with drink, just philosophical. Things fall into perspective. 'Right, Zoe. What's your game? Let's put our cards on the table. I'm not good enough for your posh pals. Am I right? Admit it. I'm really just another tramp to you, a suitable case for treatment from the soup-kitchen of the heart. A bit of interesting slumming for you? Well, it's no deal, honey. No way. You can't treat this boy like dirt. Pride's my middle name. I've always said it. Take me as you find me or leave me alone. That's the way I live. Always have, always will.

God it's 8.25! I've never been late for Zoe before!

Well, so what? I drain the last brown, bitter dregs of my Guinness. Let her wait for once. Who the hell does she think she is anyway? I step out of the warm, boozy atmosphere into the grey, pissing rain. It's coming down heavy now. I feel like diving back into the pub, but I turn up my collar and hurry across the road and just about bump into somebody coming round the corner out of Renfield Street. I'm trying to step round him, and Christ! – he's standing there in the rain greeting me. I look up. It figures. It's Dr Kichecky (or Nochecky as he's known). I haven't run into him for months, but whenever you do you can't get past him. He's this old black guy that looks and sounds a bit like Paul Robeson (an old singer my granda used to listen to), but he's a down-and-out who taps you every time he meets you. He goes through the palaver of introducing himself and telling you his cheque hasn't come through and taking your name and address to send what he owes on to you. The story goes that at one time he was a brilliant surgeon till a tragic accident happened. He sewed somebody up with the scalpel still inside them or something and then, through the disgrace, he went down the hill with the drink. It sounds like a Dr Kildare script to me. He has that look of a lifetime loser. Anyway, that's his existence now, padding about the city in an old navy raincoat and his shoes tied round with string and always carrying the same old, cracked, black attaché case.

It's a bit of a joke, bumping into him when I'm on my way to meet Zoe. I shove ten pence into his hand and try to get past him.

But the notebook's out and he's barring my way with, 'Now where shall I send the money when my cheque comes through?'

'Send it to Oxfam!' I shout, and as I turn away I catch a glimpse of his notebook, crammed with pencil-written names and addresses and amounts. And God above us, there it is, sticking out a mile at the bottom of the grubby page: Zoe's name. I crane round to see it. He snaps the book shut, but it was there definitely: Zoe's name and address and, next to it, 'amount – two pounds'.

'You've done it now!' I whisper at him, menacingly.

'What . . . what do you mean?'

'Zoe! That's what. You're in her power now, one of her debtors. If that cheque doesn't come through at last . . . God help you.'

I walk away from him, laughing out loud, and he stands staring after me as if I'm nuts.

The rain's torrential now. People are scattering off the street into doorways. And there's Zoe, standing in the door of the Odeon waiting for me, her next customer. She's wearing the creamy coat and the mauve shoes with the matching bag, and she's looking at her watch as I square my shoulders and walk up to her. She seems a bit worried, but as soon as she sees me she turns on the smile which, however, falters a bit as I stumble over the kerb.

'Gerry,' she says, knitting her brows and looking at me in that patronizing way, as if I've come out in my true down-and-out colours at last, 'are you drunk?' I'm standing there, swaying slightly, but smiling through the rain and trying to act casual.

'Maybe we'd better go and get you something to eat so you can sober up,' she says, and the Bearsden accent sounds so thick you could cut it with a knife.

'Sober up? What do you mean? I've only had a couple of drinks. Christ! You think I was like that guy in The Happy Moon. Forget it! Let's go in and see the picture.'

'We've missed about twenty minutes of it now,' she says, glancing at her watch.

'Ach well, who cares? They're always slow at the beginning, anyhow. You can pick up the threads as we go along. Come on.'

I take her by the elbow and we step towards the foyer, but she stops. She's looking down, her lips pursed.

'Look, Gerry, I don't think I would enjoy the film now. Perhaps we could see it another night. Why can't we just go for a hamburger or something?'

I step back from her.

'Oh you wouldn't enjoy it, eh? The odour of the alcohol would spoil the pleasure of the Odeon? How awful! Let's go and sort Gerry out first. Stick his head in the horse trough and maybe get him shaved and deloused as well.'

It's all coming out now. All the stuff that was gathering in me in the pub.

Zoe's never heard me speaking like this before. She's looking at me, wide-eyed, and glancing about as if she could do with some help in such strange circumstances.

'That's not very fair, Gerry. After all, you're half an hour late and it's not my fault —'

'Half an hour late! Christ!' I turn my eyes up to the roof and give full vent to the sarcasm. 'Oh how awful! Oh what a big crime! Half an hour late for the hand-out. It's like trying to make your signing on time: "Right, just wait till the queue's through. Now then, explain why you're late. We may have to lapse your payments for this, you know. We have other people to attend to and we can't just run this office to suit you." Come on, Zoe. Get your head out the buttercups. This is the real world!'

'Gerry, what's the matter?' It's an urgent whisper, and there's a pained look in her face. 'Why are you being so aggressive?'

'Aggressive? Who's being aggressive? This is me trying to get you to come clean. Admit the truth. See the facts for what they are. I've let it all wash over me for too long. Well, that's it. I've had a bellyful. I'm putting up with no more indignities!'

It was a good word. I spat it out.

'Indignities? What on earth do you mean, Gerry? What are you talking about?' She's really wide-eyed now and there's a line in the middle of her forehead.

'Oh don't give us that! What do you think I've got, skin or an elephant's hide? I'm not daft, you know. I can see what you're doing. Every time you venture out of Bearsden it's a visit to the slums, an expedition to study the natives. You bring your bag of coloured beads and hand them out if we say something nice. Oh, they're good chaps really, these people, if you know how to treat them right.'

'Gerry, please –'

'Oh don't give me any more of your crap! That's the way you've treated me all along. Just the same as the rest. Just another tramp you're taking an interest in: a donation to Oxfam, a night out with Gerry. Does it all go in the diary at night? Good works done among the lower orders today: pictures with Gerry (required detoxification first); two pounds to Dr Nochecky, an old dilapidated Negro who reminded me of *Uncle Tom's Cabin*.'

'How did you know –'

'Oh we've got a network, you know. The subculture. We're all one big tribe in this city, the lower orders. We report back at night too, pool all the takings, everything we get off the white bwanas.'

I'm in full swing now. Pouring it all out like vomit. Zoe looks stunned.

'Gerry, I don't know how you can say all this,' she says, shaking her head. She sighs and hesitates then, turning up the collar of her coat, she says briskly, 'Anyway, I think I'd better go home now. Goodnight!' and ducks out into the rain.

'It's true. That's how I can say it,' I yell, striding after her. 'It's all been a big freak show to you, hasn't it? Everybody you met when you were with me . . . the old lady, the whole lot. You couldn't wait to make an expedition to the scheme. Never mind if the smell would have made you puke. Your curiosity would have got you there.'

Zoe has stopped. We're facing each other in the pouring rain.

'Oh yes, and what about Gerry all this time? Invite Gerry out to Bearsden? Bloody Bearsden! No way! He might dirty the avenues. Don't take your work home with you. Just visit them in their own patch and observe them. As if we were a bunch of bloody savages!'

And then, I remember, Zoe looks at me as she's never done before.

Her face is white and she's staring hard at me, but saying nothing. It's as if she's seeing me for the first time. I can't think of anything else to say and Zoe just stands there not bothering about the rain.

When she finally speaks, it's almost a whisper.

'How can you be so cruel?' She pauses as if she might get an answer. 'I never invited you out to my house because I felt absolutely certain you wouldn't want to come.' She pauses again, but I still can't think of anything to say. 'If you stop to think of it for one moment, you'll realize that I've never once suggested anywhere we went. Never once. And I've always thought that was the best arrangement. Whatever made you happy was always good enough for me. And any time you've looked unhappy, I've always thought it was me that was doing something wrong, though I've never known what.' It's still the same whisper, but her voice is shaky now. 'As for your mother, I thought she was a delightful person. I would have liked to have met her again. How horrible of you to suggest I was looking down on her! How could you think that? But what's worse is that all this time . . . all the time you've been going out with me, you've had this awful, poisoned idea of me in your head, and you've never said anything about it. It makes me feel so sad, I . . . and all the time, I've been just so pleased to be with you – maybe a bit uneasy sometimes, no wonder, I see now – but really very pleased to be going out with you, and . . . Oh, Gerry, how could you be so cruel and so . . . so unfair?'

Her lip's quivering. 'Wait a minute, Zoe . . .'

'No, I won't wait,' she says, stepping away from me as if

she's suddenly discovered I've got rabies. 'I'm going home now and I never want to see you again.'

God! Tears are running down her face!

'Zoe . . .' I move towards her, but she turns and walks away.

She turns back. 'Here! I don't want to keep anything you ever gave me!'

She's opening her bag. Christ! What's coming? I never gave her anything. She throws it at my feet in the rain. It's the folded up picture the Artist did of her. She runs off down into the bright lights and noise of Renfield Street, hunched up, her hands stuck in her coat pockets.

'Zoe! . . . Zoe!' I'm shouting, lurching down the road after her, the Artist's picture clutched in my hand. I collide with somebody running with his head down through the bucketing rain. I stagger on. Zoe's jumping on a bus at the lights – not her bus – any bus to get away from me!

'Zoe! . . . Zoe!' The lights have changed and I'm running full belt as the bus revs away. I'm almost there. I'm reaching for the bar just as the driver shuts the door. I trip and fall into the path of a car gathering speed behind the bus. There's a screech of brakes like a cry of alarm and a scream from the pavement, and I roll over into the gutter as Zoe's bus disappears down the road out of sight.

I'm on my hands and knees watching it. An old couple are shuffling past, arm in arm.

'A young fella the worse for drink, Isa,' comments the old guy without looking at me.

I limp away back up through the sodden city and end up in a corner in some nondescript, old man's boozer, I don't know where, drinking the last of my week's money.

The next morning hit me on the head like a ton of cold water. My guts contracted every time an image from the night before came to the surface. I stuck my head in the pan and put my fingers down my throat and spewed. It must have been a bad pint, I told the old lady. 'Well, you will drink,' she says.

If this was one of those *True Romance* stories or something out of the *Jackie*, I would tell you how the truth about Zoe now emerged like suppressed evidence after a rigged trial. It would all come out with a rush: how Zoe had never been out with a boy before me; how her father was a drunkard who used to batter Zoe and her mother; how he's now offsky down to England, leaving their lives in ruins after they've been virtual prisoners in the Bearsden bungalow for years; how Zoe rebuilds their lives, tending the mother, who's now a physical and mental wreck, with constant loving care; how they've got hardly a penny to live on; how Zoe meets a boy she thinks is wonderful because he takes her to restaurants and gets her portrait done and so on; how I realize I've thrown away a pearl, but it's too late now, or is it?

As you'll know, life's never really like that, but, as the days went by it came home to me that what I actually knew about Zoe you could have written on the back of a stamp. And then one day when I met Dunky and the girlfriend and I started hearing things about Zoe that sounded as if they might just have a vague resemblance to that *True Romance* story, I made an excuse and hurried away, shuddering, in case the whole thing would come true.

There were many phone calls to Zoe, but she didn't want to know. Her old lady answered in a clipped tone: Zoe was not available. Or the phone was put down as soon as I spoke. She couldn't even bear to speak to me. I was unforgiveable. I even wrote, but she didn't reply. It was dead, the whole thing. I've never seen Zoe since.

So here I am, a year later, back in The South Pacific hoping for what, I don't know. The Artist is plying his trade with a baldy, middle-aged guy who looks like a shabby office clerk out for his lunch-break. He's forking chips into his mouth and reading his paper, while the Artist sketches.

'Now, what colour are your eyes, sir?'

'Bloodshot.'

A moment's nervous hesitation of the Artist's fingers over the pencil pocket. 'Oh, don't say that,' he says, pulling out the blue and finishing the sketch.

'That's nothing like me,' says the clerk, glancing up from his *Daily Express*. 'It's more like Humpty Dumpty with a moustache, for God's sake.'

'Well, that's the way the Artist sees you.'

'Here! Scram!' The clerk pushes fifty pence across the table. The Artist tips his hat and departs with his money.

The drawing falls over the edge of the table and floats down on to the floor. The old clerk goes back to his dinner and his paper.

At Central Station

EDWIN MORGAN

At Central Station, in the middle of the day,
a woman is pissing on the pavement.
With her back to the wall and her legs spread
she bends forward, her hair over her face,
the drab skirt and coat not even hitched up.
Her water hits the stone with force
and streams across into the gutter.
She is not old, not young either,
not dirty, yet hardly clean,
not in rags, but going that way.
She stands at the city centre, skeleton at the feast.
Executives off the London train

start incredulously but jump the river
and meekly join their taxi queue.
The Glasgow crowd hurries past,
hardly looks, or hardly dares to look,
or looks hard, bold as brass, as
the poet looks, not bold as brass
but hard, swift, slowing his walk
a little, accursed recorder, his feelings
as confused as the November leaves.
She is a statue in a whirlpool,
beaten about by nothing he can give words to,

bleeding into the waves of talk
and traffic awful ichors of need.
Only two men frankly stop,
grin broadly, throw a gibe at her
as they cross the street to the betting-shop.
Without them the indignity,
the dignity, would be incomplete.

Staff of Life

ARTHUR YOUNG

During the depression my father was idle. While my mother worked to keep us he ran a garden allotment, to fill his empty days, to help with food and to salve his self-respect.

It was my job to gather dung.

In the summer mornings while he bent to his weeding and hoeing, I made designs with the white chuckies which outlined the various beds; or made a wee house out of seedling boxes. Come midday we ate, sitting just inside the door of the hut which he had patiently built from boxes and old wood.

After dinner, before settling to his only pipe of the day, he would cut the heel and leaf from a stalk of red rhubarb for me. Then he puffed away, while I scrunched contentedly, dipping the end in a little poke of sugar before every bite, grooing in tart delight if I had not coated it well enough.

Soon, when his cronies came by to play solo or dominoes for spent matchsticks, they laughed at me and said it would keep me regular.

Then to be rid of me I was sent for dung, to make the flowers smell and keep the rhubarb red.

I went with Dougie Crawford, the son of one of my father's friends. He was twice my age and had a bogie.

We went to the Stey Brae, to the tracing station. On the way there I got a hurl, hunkering down on the bogie, feet on an upturned shovel. We jumbled over cobbles; swayed round corners; jinked in and out of the traffic, clear across the town to the Brae.

This hill, notorious for its steepness and twists, had running its whole length a pathway of cross-laid granite setts, to help horses keep their feet and give them purchase. At the bottom, the town council had sited a tracing station.

In a stable, by the side of the road, they kept half a dozen powerful horses. On payment of a fee by a carter, one of these would be hitched, tandem, to a heavy load, and the two horses, led by a trace boy, would plod, steaming and snorting, to the head of the hill.

Of course, the stable was a great howff. It was ruled by two ostlers, men with seamed leathery faces, who wore leggings and aprons of sacking. They had ponderous bellies, girt about with broad brass-studded leather belts. They swore at the beasts with hoarse crooning voices; roystering oaths which, I realized later, were really little songs of love.

The place would be full of drivers and carters. There would be joking, and pipe-reek, and spitting, and drinking from quart bottles of ale, while the horses were yoked and loused; fed and groomed.

The traffic on the hill was of all kinds: brewers' drays, coal lorries, grain floats, furniture pantechnicons, contractors' carts – all pulled by big, patient horses, mostly Clydesdales. There was the odd Percheron, Shire or Punch, but they weren't a patch on our local-bred beauties.

Naturally, the six trace horses were Clydesdales too. Our favourite was Hector.

Nobly named, he was the biggest by far, and was superb to see with his creamy mane against his chestnut coat, and his feet, big as pie ashets, with their silky white-fringed spats.

You can imagine our plunder was bountiful. Dougie was

on to the droppings in a flash, scooping them into the bogie.
Somehow, Hector's offering seemed special, as with utter
disdain of the smelly, petrol-driven vehicles all about him,
with their stinking exhausts, he lifted his tail and gave out
great golden gobs of steaming ordure.

When we returned home, I trotted beside Dougie, holding
on to his belt. As we ran we inhaled the sharp ammonia
smell of our treasure.

One day a trace boy, sent for tobacco, had dawdled; was
not on hand when needed.

The ostler swore.

'Whaur's yon bluidy boy got tae?'

'Can Ah go?' asked Dougie, bold and scared together.

By this time we were kenspeckle.

'Ah believe ye micht!'

Pop-eyed with pride, he took the trace bridle in his hand,
then held out the other for me.

'He can come too, eh no?' he asked.

Was there ever such a hero, to remember a halfling like me
in that moment of his own glory.

'Weel – ! See and haud oan tae him ticht!'

For, of course, the real reward of being a trace boy was the
return journey – on the back of the horse.

We had Hector, our own beauty. He hauled the load to
the top with ease, then waited patiently while the carter
hefted us up on to his broad back.

Dougie held on to the big leather collar, his knuckles
showing white, with me locked between his arms. Greatly
daring he dug his heels into the broad flanks. Hector
obediently went forward in a slow canter.

We had so often watched the trace boys with envy, that
we had never considered the danger.

The huge back was frighteningly high above the cobbles.

The motion was sudden and jerky. The smooth hard coat was as slippery as glass.

Somehow we reached the other end and were helped down. Our terror turned immediately to pride and joy. Our happiness knew no limits at our own daring and success.

So the summer progressed. The flowers never smelt sweeter. The rhubarb was never so red: and I was never so regular.

When summer ended, I went to school for the first time. The allotment was forgotten in November fogs and December frosts.

There was snow, I remember, just before Christmas. One Saturday, late in the afternoon, Dougie appeared in tackety boots and a Balaclava helmet.

'Comin' tae see Hector?' he asked.

'Will I no' just!' I cried.

Without the bogie this time, we dodged along the pavements through the throng of shoppers. The winter wind dirled in my ears and to my intense excitement, before we were long on the way, it started to snow hard. This added the final touch to the twinkle of street lights in early darkness, and the bustle and smells of Christmas. I remember feeling so happy.

Landing on roads already surfaced by packed icy snow, the huge swirling flakes soon formed a muffling carpet. The heavy traffic and the countless feet pounded it hard and slippery. By the time we reached the tracing stable the Stey Brae had been converted into a dangerous glacis, under which the granite setts were buried and useless, despite attempts at clearing and sanding.

We soon caught an anxious undertone to the rough

voices for no man wanted to get in the way of the great, pounding, steel-shod hooves as they fought for surety and balance.

'Yin o' they beasts will gang doon afore ye're a' din!' warned one of the ostlers. 'They'll hae tae come aff. It's no' safe ony mair.'

But the carters already there were late and weary and wanted to get done.

'Weel! Yin mair raik an' then it's feenish!' he decreed.

Dougie and I waited confidently beside our bonny giant. He would show them.

He did too.

Stepping like the prince he was, he drove his way up the hill, hauling the yoked horse and load behind him. Dougie and I ran alongside shouting his praises.

On looking back, what made the next happening so horrifying was the incongruous silence. There was no warning horn, no squeal of brakes or tyres, no shout: just the light-beam, grotesquely out of place, shining across the road instead of down as a car slid out of control on one of the bends.

There wasn't even a very big bump, but the momentum and lack of friction underfoot was enough to sweep the cart and the two horses backwards.

For one frozen moment Hector stood his ground four-square, until inexorably his head was pulled up, back and over. At the last moment he tried to roll sideways but his huge frame was never meant for such contortions.

'Christ! The bluidy beast is coupit,' was the agonized shout.

Then the noise started, obscene in its shrill terror. Hector lay flailing on the ground, his teeth gnashing, his eyes rolling in agony, his screams human and mortal. Jagged slivers of white bone sticking from the shin showed where the bone of the leg was broken.

One of the ostlers arrived, purple in the face.

'Aa Christ! Christ! The puir bluidy beast!'

The cry went up for a gun or for the knackers, but shaking his head the ostler drew out a horn-handled clasp knife. Opening out the big blade, he held it cupped in his hand, so that the sharp point lay sheltered and directed along his middle finger. He soothed the pain-wracked animal enough to get near it.

To my utter astonishment he lifted its tail and plunged hand, knife and arm up to the elbow into the pouting dark orifice.

'Whit's he daein' up its airse, mister?' Dougie pulled at a man's coat in alarm.

'There's a big vein in there, son. He'll puncture it, and the beast will soon be quated.'

Then more kindly: 'It'll no' hurt.'

His words seemed true, for a few minutes after the ostler brought his hand away, dripping red, the great horse quietened. His head settled and he began to breathe in ever slowing gasps.

At the end his bowels gave way and skailed a great, reeking puddle of blood in the snow, where it steamed and congealed and turned black.

I felt my head go round.

'Dougie! Take me home!'

I remember nothing of the return trip. Indeed I remember little of the next few months, except that even in those days of tight money, the doctor was called to see me.

The last time I saw Dougie Crawford was just after the start of the war.

He was a pasty-faced private in the Argylls, with black holes in his teeth and a fag stuck on his lower lip. He was killed in Malaya.

The Stey Brae has disappeared. It has been bulldozed, straightened and smoothed into a gently curving four lane highway. Even now I can go to where Hector died.

I still get rhubarb too; sometimes with custard. But it is pale, anaemic stuff, with chlorotic leaves. They tell me it is produced in some foreign part. No doubt it is forced under glass and fed on chemical concoctions.

It only gives me wind.

Fat Girl's Confession

LIZ LOCHHEAD

Roll up and see the Fat Lady!
Such a jolly sight to see.
Seems my figure is a Figure of Fun . . .
to everyone but me.

Smile! Say Cottage Cheese!
You all know me –
I'm the Office Fat Girl, the one you see
wearing Vast Dark Dresses and a Cheery Veneer . . .
and lingerie constructed by a civil engineer.

Occasionally, you meet some bloke who'll give you this
    tripe
about how, YEUCH, he's repelled by the skinny model
    type.
He CAN'T see the attraction, he'll swear by all he owns
it'd be like lying in bed with a rickle of bones.
But, o how he LURRVES
yer Voluptuous Curves
and your Supper Board that Groans.

I met him at my wee cousin's wedding – he was the Best
    Man – he says to me
would you like to go out for a bite to eat? I mean, do you
    fancy a curry?
A Chinese? An Italian? I said, who me? Oh, I love

lasagne and canne-linguini and PASTA and stuff.
(well, who with pasta, ever says *basta*,
enough!)
And then for my MAIN course I tend to choose
something smothered in a sauce made of butter, cream and
    booze
with asparagus hollandaise and cauliflower mornay
potatoes dauphines, onion rings and mushrooms sauté.
And after the cheeseboard, my sweet tooth's nagging, so
I need another great big stodgy wedge of Black Forest
    Gâteau.
Well, when it comes to pudding,
the way I see it –
with cheesecake you've a choice:
either EAT it or BE it.

I didnae cry when he left me.
I gave not one cheep, not a chirrup –
just devoured a whole packet of Mr Kipling Kunzle Cakes
and a half-hundredweight sack of Mexicali Taco Chips
    dunked in maple syrup,
went for a double blackpudding supper, then half an hour
    later,
I ravished the refrigerator
(in my classic response to Rejection and Pain)
and immediately began eating
my Heart Out again.

But, Oh
Dear Joe,
much as I miss you
I just been reading how Fat Is A Feminist Issue.

Fat Girls like me have all fallen from grace . . .
if I could feed my own ego I wouldnae need to feed my
    face!
Everyone needs Oral Satisfaction, but
the Truly Fulfilled don't need a filled-full gut.
I says, Enough of this junk food, you are what you eat.
When did you last see your lover?
When did you last see your feet?
So . . . I'm persevering, but it's kind of hard
to live on lettuce, and self-regard.

But, you know, I've been really, really, really good today!
Breakfast was black coffee, plus a saccharine tab from the
    tube.
For my lunch, a half-a-cup of chicken boullion
made with a Knorr chicken-stock cube.
Dinner: two slices of starch-reduced Ryvita
with a scrape of slimmer's imitation margarine,
then I pedalled myself blue in the face on the Exercise
    Machine.
See, I've joined this Health Club, and hell, I
saw some sights you wouldnae believe!
Enough heaving flesh to make you heave.
All that pummelling, and pedalling, and pounding, and
    sweating,
and keeking in the mirror to see how much thinner you're
    getting!
Well, there's not one lady waging the Inch War or wielding
    the tape
who doesnae wish for a Dishy Man to lick her inty shape.

So I'm stuck here in this Stephanie Bowman Sweat-It-Off
    Slimmersuit.
I feel a right clown!
I'm to huff, I'm to puff,
I'll WEAR my hips down.
I'll mortify my surplus flesh,
remove it like a tumour . . .
and all to make of myself the kind of confection
who'll appeal to the Consumer?

The New Boy

GEDDES THOMSON

Tam was in a good mood that morning. His mum had had a big win at the bingo the night before. She had brought home some special fish suppers, two bottles of Irn Bru and a big red box of chocolates. A nice surprise on a Tuesday night with the rain running down the windows, no money for the gas fire and the telly rotten as usual.

She had given Tam five one pound notes which now nestled in his jerkin pocket. It was a great feeling, pound notes in your pocket. He would pass the day thinking about what he would do with all that money. Better than listening to moany old teachers.

He was explaining all this to his mate, Alec, as they dragged their feet through the school gate, when he first saw the new boy.

Tam nudged Alec. 'Whose zat?'

'Doan know. Never seen im before.'

The new boy was surrounded by a crowd of first years. He was a big broad-shouldered lad with a sun-tanned face and dark curly hair. He was dressed in a fancy pullover and brown corduroys and he was wearing a tie. The first years seemed to be enjoying his company, because they were laughing and skipping about him like a pack of playful dogs.

Tam stopped and stared at the newcomer in *his* play-ground. He didn't like the way the first years were listening to the new boy's every word. Tam was used to younger boys looking up to *him* as a kind of leader.

'Hullo,' shouted the new boy.

'Talking tae me, son, or chewin a brick?' Tam shouted back.

The first years stopped their capering and edged away like cowboys in a western when the goodie and the baddie meet up in the saloon. The new boy was suddenly alone which didn't seem to bother him one little bit.

'Braw mornin,' he said.

'*Braw Morning!*' Tam imitated. 'Who the hell ur you? Oor Wullie or somethin? Listen. We rule here, pal. Don't forget it. O K?'

Just then the bell went. The playground began to empty. Tam turned away and swaggered towards the technical block. He felt the crinkly pound notes in his pocket.

Tam didn't see the new boy again till the second last period of the morning – English. It was one of his better subjects. Mr Campbell wasn't as moany as the other teachers and there wasn't anything special to learn in English.

'Seasy,' he told Alec. 'Ah kin speak it, can't ah? No like that bloody French. Ivrybody should talk English. Wan languidge fur ivrybody.'

Alec decided there must be something wrong with that argument. 'Yiv goat tae huv different languidges. It's their culture n'at. How are aw the foreigners gonny learn English?'

Tam didn't answer because a snobby girl prefect with gold braid on her blazer had just brought in the new boy.

'See whit the cat's dragged in,' he whispered to Alec. 'Big heid the breid.'

The new boy was nearly as tall as Mr Campbell. He

THE OTHER SIDE OF THE CLYDE

looked perfectly relaxed and smiled broadly, not the slight shy smile of an ordinary new pupil. Mr Campbell directed him to a seat at the back of the room beside Kathy Milligan.

They were doing a project about advertising. It was called 'The Hidden Persuaders'. Mr Campbell always had fancy titles like that for his English projects. But Tam quite liked him and usually he weighed in with a few answers just to keep him happy.

Today Mr Campbell was on about TV adverts, asking the class for their favourites. Tam, aware of the new boy somewhere behind him, put up his hand.

'Ah like the one about biscuits, Sir.'

Mr Campbell smiled encouragingly.

'Tell us about it, Tom.'

'Well it's these Mexican bandits an they rob a bank an the federales come an it's fur this biscuit.'

'I know the one you mean. Why do you like it?'

Tam decided to show off, show the new boy how gallus he was.

'Well, ah like the burds, Sir. Lovely burds in that ad.'

Alec spluttered with laughter, but Mr Campbell was not so easily put off. 'Why do they have – young ladies – in the advert?'

There was a pause. 'Yes, Colin?'

Tam heard the voice of the new boy behind him. 'It's tae mak ye think the product is ... glamorous. Tae ... tae connect it wae nice ideas so that ye'll gae oot an buy it.'

Everybody turned round to look. They realized that he had put into words what had been vaguely going through their own minds.

Mr Campbell was delighted. 'That's a very good answer, Colin. A *very* good answer.'

But Colin wasn't finished yet. 'Tak this lassie aside me,

Sir. Now if she was tae recommend biscuits oan the TV, I wid definitely buy them because she looks sae nice.'

Tam narrowed his eyes and glared. Kathy Milligan's dark head was lowered, but he could see her blush and smile. He had quite fancied Kathy Milligan for a long time and here was this character giving her the patter already.

Tam was never sure how to deal with girls. Once, in the corridor, he had smiled at Kathy Milligan and punched her on the arm.

'Why did you do that?' Alec had asked.

'Ah – like er.'

'You *like* er!' Alec had laughed. 'Ye've goat a funny way a showin it. What would ye do if ye *didny* like er? Break er arm?'

Alec was nudging him. 'This guy's quite a character, Tam!'

Tam stared at Alec and chose his words carefully. 'This guy,' he said, 'is a *snob* an a *swot* and ah'm gonny sort him out.'

'He's big.'

'Aye, a big drip. Wears a tie, talks funny, gies good answers. He's a big,' Tam stopped, searching for the word that would sum up what he felt about the new boy. 'He's a big tube.'

'Kathy Milligan likes im.'

Tam suddenly realized that his so-called pal, Alec, was deliberately annoying him and didn't answer.

For the rest of the period he day-dreamed about how he would sort out the new boy.

The last period of the morning was PE. Once again the new boy was in his class. Tam watched him closely in the dressing-room and nudged Alec when the new boy took a pair of shining white shorts out of his duffle bag.

93

'Look whit snobby's goat.'

Tam wore his own black shorts under his jeans. He never carried anything to school, even a pencil. If you tried to carry things around they just got lost. And then there was trouble.

'Ah still think e's big.' It was Alec again. Sometimes Tam wondered why he bothered with Alec, because Alec wasn't normal. He supported Partick Thistle for a start. Partick Thistle!

Tam decided to needle his friend. 'See me an him. It'll be like Rangers and Partick Thistle. Nae contest. The bigger they are, the harder they faw.'

The PE teacher, Mr Simpson, appeared, bouncing a football on the stone floor. Big Sim he was called and he was as hard as nails. That was why Tam never forgot his shorts.

'OK,' Big Sim said. 'Pay attention, lads. Football in the top playground and nothing above head height because of the windows. Got that?'

Big Sim's cold blue eyes flicked over them, one by one, looking for any boy without his full kit, but even wee Sammy, who didn't know the day of the week, had brought his gear.

Out in the playground they were divided into teams. Tam was pleased to see that he was in the opposite team from the new boy. Now he would show him who was the boss.

The game started. The orange football began to skid around the playground chased by the players.

After a few minutes the new boy, who turned out to be a good player, dribbled towards Tam. As he went past Tam tripped him, making it look like an accidental late tackle. The new boy fell his full length on the concrete playground. His nose was in a puddle and his knee was bleeding. The white shorts were splattered with mud.

Big Sim came pounding up, blowing his whistle and

waving his arms like a big time referee as the boys crowded round the figure on the ground.

'Get back, you lot. Are you OK lad? Any damage?'

The new boy smiled. 'Ah'm fine, Sir. Ah've just skint ma knee. That's aw. Accidents happen, ye ken.'

But Tam sensed that the rest of them didn't think it was an accident. He heard Alec's whisper over his left shoulder: 'See you. You're mental!'

For the rest of the game he hardly got a kick at the ball, but the new boy's name began to ring out over the playground.

'Well done, Colin.'

'Nice pass, Colin.'

'Great goal, Colin.'

Afterwards, in the dressing-room, Tam pulled on his clothes without a word to anybody. He felt that somehow he had suffered a great defeat and he wasn't quite sure how it had happened. OK, he had tripped the guy. So what? That was nothing.

Five minutes later Tam sat in the shelter and watched the entrance of the PE building. He felt a tension that tightened his throat and neck so that he could hardly breathe.

At last he saw the new boy come out the glass doors and look around as if searching for something. Or someone.

Tam rose to his feet in the dark shelter. Slowly he walked out into the sunlight. The new boy saw him. He was waving something in his hand.

'Can ah see ye a meenit?' he shouted in that funny accent which grated on Tam's nerves.

'Ah suppose you can,' Tam shouted back, 'unless you're blind.'

The new boy was now standing in front of him. Alec was right. He *was* big. Tam had to look up into the broad brown face.

'The bigger they are the harder they faw.' That was what he had told Alec. It had been a favourite saying of his father's. 'The bigger they are the harder they faw.'

Tam clenched his fists inside his jerkin pockets.

'Something wrang?' the new boy asked.

'Aye,' Tam said. '*You*'re wrang. You've been wrang since the minute ah saw ye. Who *are* you? Where do you come fae?'

The new boy opened his mouth to answer and, at that moment, Tam jumped him in a flurry of swirling arms and thudding fists. He heard the new boy gasp in pain, but he also felt knuckles crash into his own face. Desperately, he grabbed his enemy round the waist and the two of them swayed and tottered round the playground like two drunk men until they crashed to the ground.

Tam had him locked round the waist in a vice-like grip, but the new boy had an equally strong hold on Tam's neck.

After a minute like this he heard Colin MacDonald say, 'You let me go and ah'll let *you* go.'

Tam strengthened his grip while he thought about this. It might be a trick. On the other hand Tam could feel his strength slowly draining away. He decided he had better take the offer while there was still time.

'One – two – three!' And Tam let go and at the same moment felt the arms drop away from his own neck.

They lay side by side on the hard playground. Exhausted.

'Yer a bonny fighter,' he heard the new boy say.

'Yer no sae bad, yersel,' Tam had to admit.

'Oh an ah've goat something fur ye,' Colin MacDonald sat up and opened his big brown fist to reveal a heap of green paper. 'Ah fund them in the dressing-room. They're yours, aren't they? Ah wis comin tae gie them tae yi.'

The pound notes. No longer new and crinkly, but crushed and dirty.

They grinned at each other.

Glasgow October 1972

EDWIN MORGAN

At the Old Ship Bank pub in Saltmarket
a milk-lapping contest is in progress.
A dozen very assorted Bridgeton cats
have sprung from their starting-blocks
to get their heads down in the gleaming saucers.
In the middle of the picture
young Tiny is about to win his bottle of whisky
by kittening through the sweet half-gill
in one minute forty seconds flat, but
Sarah, at the end of the line,
self-contained and silver-grey,
has sat down with her back to the saucer
and surveys the photographers calmly.
She is a cat who does not like milk.

Brisbane November 1972

EDWIN MORGAN

In this sharp close-up
of a young man's foot,
the centre of attention
is a large blister
where he had cut himself
swimming in a lake.
Swimming in the lake
of the blister is
a half-inch fish.
It noses inquisitively
against the thin soft walls
as the surgeon's needle
approaches from the world
of air to release it
and its gasping thimble-
ful of life.

London August 1972

EDWIN MORGAN

At the Eastman Dental Hospital
a homely hornbill in a white coat
is having an acrylic upper bill
fitted over the stub of a broken beak.
He sits quietly, with a steady eye
on the nurse who holds him. Soon
he will snap hard plastic against hard horn,
and eat at last – not the dentist's hand.

Away in Airdrie

JAMES KELMAN

During the early hours of the morning the boy was awakened by wheezing, spluttering noises and the smell of a cigarette burning. The blankets hoisted up and the body rolled under, knocking him over on to his brother. And the feet were freezing, an icy draught seemed to come from them. Each time he woke from then on he could either smell the cigarette or see the sulphur head of the match flaring in the dark. When he opened his eyes for the final time the man was sitting up in bed and coughing out: Morning Danny boy, how's it going?

I knew it was you.

Aye, my feet I suppose. Run through and get me a drink of water son will you.

Uncle Archie could make people laugh at breakfast, even Danny's father – but still he had to go to work. He said, If you'd told me you were coming I could've made arrangements.

Ach, I was wanting to surprise yous all. Uncle Archie grinned: You'll be coming to the match afterwards though eh?

The father looked at him.

The boys're through at Airdrie the day.

Aw aye, aye. The father nodded, then he shrugged. If you'd told me earlier Archie – by the time I'm finished work and that . . .

Uncle Archie was smiling: Come on, long time since we went to a match the gether. And you're rare and handy for a train here as well.

Aye I know that but eh; the father hesitated. He glanced at the other faces round the table. He said, Naw Archie. I'll have to be going to my work and that, the gaffer asked me in specially. And I don't like knocking him back, you know how it is.

Ach, come on –

Honest, and by the time I finish it'll be too late. Take the boys but. Danny – Danny'll go anywhere for a game.

Uncle Archie nodded for a moment. How about it lads?

Not me, replied Danny's brother. I've got to go up the town.

Well then . . . Uncle Archie paused and smiled: Me and you Danny boy, eh!

Aye Uncle Archie. Smashing.

Here! – I thought you played the game yourself on Saturdays?

No, the father said, I mean aye – but it's just the mornings he plays, eh Danny?

Aye. Aw that'll be great Uncle Archie. I've never been to Broomfield.

It's no a bad wee park.

Danny noticed his mother was looking across the table at his father while she rose to tidy away the breakfast stuff. He got up and went to collect his football gear from the room. The father also got up, he pulled on his working coat and picked his parcel of sandwiches from the top of the sideboard. When the mother returned from the kitchen he kissed her on the cheek and said he would be home about half past two, and added: See you when you get back Archie. Hope the game goes the right way.

No fear of that! We'll probably take five off them. Uncle Archie grinned, You'll be kicking yourself for no coming — best team we've had in years.

Ach well, Danny'll tell me all about it. Okay then . . . he turned to leave. Cheerio everybody.

The outside door closed. Uncle Archie remained by himself at the table. After a moment the mother brought him an ashtray and lifted the saucer he had been using in its stead. He said, Sorry Betty.

You're smoking too heavy.

I know. I'm trying to . . . He stopped; Danny had come in carrying a tin of black polish and a brush, his football-boots beneath his arm. As he laid the things in front of the fireplace he asked: You seen my jersey mum?

It's where it should be.

The bottom drawer?

She looked at him. He had sat down on the carpet and was taking the lid off the tin of black polish. She waited until he placed an old newspaper under the things, before leaving the room.

Hey Danny, called the Uncle. You needing any supporters this morning?

Supporters?

Aye, I'm a hell of a good shouter you know. Eh, wanting me along?

Well . . .

What's up? Uncle Archie grinned.

Glancing up from the book he was reading Danny's brother snorted: He doesn't play any good when people's watching.

Rubbish, cried Danny, it's not that at all. It's just that — the car Uncle Archie, see we go in the teacher's car and there's hardly any space.

With eleven players and the driver! Uncle Archie laughed: I'm no surprised.

But I'll be back in plenty of time for the match, he said as he began brushing the first boot.

Aye well you better because I'll be off my mark at half twelve pronto. Mind now.

Aye.

It's yes, said the mother while coming into the room, she was carrying two cups of fresh tea for herself and Uncle Archie.

Danny was a bit embarrassed, walking with his uncle along the road, and over the big hill leading out from the housing scheme, down towards the railway station in Old Drumchapel. But he met nobody. And there was nothing wrong with the scarf his uncle was wearing, it just looked strange at first, the blue and white, really different from the Rangers' blue. But supporters of a team were entitled to wear its colours. It was better once the train had stopped at Queen Street Station. Danny was surprised to see so many of them all getting on, and hearing their accents. In Airdrie Uncle Archie became surrounded by a big group of them, all laughing and joking. They were passing round a bottle and opening cans of beer.

Hey Danny boy come here a minute! Uncle Archie reached out to grip him by the shoulder, taking him into the middle of the group. See this yin, he was saying: He'll be playing for Rangers in next to no time ... The men stared down at him. Aye, went on his uncle, scored two for the school this morning. Man of the Match.

That a fact son? called a man.

Danny reddened.

You're joking! cried Uncle Archie. Bloody ref chalked another three off him for offside! Eh Danny?

Danny was trying to free himself from the grip, to get out of the group.

Another man was chuckling: Ah well son you can forget all about the Rangers this afternoon.

Aye you'll be seeing a *team* the day, grunted an old man who was wearing a bunnet with blue and white checks.

Being in Broomfield Park reminded him of the few occasions he had been inside Hampden watching the Scottish School-boys. Hollow kind of air. People standing miles away could be heard talking to each other, the same with the actual players, you could hear them grunting and calling out names. There was a wee box of a Stand that looked like it was balancing on stilts.

The halftime score was one goal apiece. Uncle Archie brought him a Bovril and a hot pie soaked in the watery brown sauce. A rare game son eh? he said.

Aye, and the best view I've ever had too.

Eat your pie.

The match had ended in a two all draw. As they left the terracing he tagged along behind the group Uncle Archie was walking in. He hung about gazing into shop-windows when the game was being discussed, not too far from the station. His uncle was very much involved in the chat and after a time he came to where Danny stood. Listen, he said, pointing across and along the road. See that cafe son? Eh, that cafe down there? Here, half a quid for you – away and buy yourself a drink of ginger and a bar of chocolate or something.

Danny nodded.

THE OTHER SIDE OF THE CLYDE

And I'll come and get you in a minute.

He took the money.

I'm just nipping in for a pint with the lads . . .

Have I to spend it all?

The lot. Uncle Archie grinned.

I'll get chips then, said Danny, but I'll go straight into the cafe and get a cup of tea after, OK?

Fair enough Danny boy fair enough. And I'll come and get you in fifteen minutes pronto. Mind and wait till I come now.

Danny nodded.

He was sitting with an empty cup for ages and the waitress was looking at him. She hovered about at his table till finally she snatched the cup out of his hands. So far he had spent twenty-five pence and he was spending no more. The remaining money was for school through the week. Out from the cafe he crossed the road, along to the pub. Whenever the door opened he peered inside. Soon he could spot his uncle, sitting at a long table, surrounded by a lot of men from the match. But it was impossible to catch his attention, and each time he tried to keep the door open a man seated just inside was kicking it shut.

He wandered along to the station, and back again, continuing on in the opposite direction; he was careful to look round every so often. Then in the doorway of the close next to the pub he lowered himself to sit on his heels. But when the next man was entering the pub Danny was on to his feet and in behind him, keeping to the rear of the man's flapping coat tails.

You ready yet Uncle Archie?

Christ Almighty look who's here.

The woman's closing the cafe.

Uncle Archie had turned to the man sitting beside him: It's the brother's boy.

Aw, the man nodded.

What's up son?

It's shut, the cafe.

Just a tick, replied Uncle Archie. He lifted the small tumbler to his lips, indicated the pint glass of beer in front of him on the table. Soon as I finish that we'll be away son. OK? I'll be out in a minute.

The foot had stretched out and booted the door shut behind him. He lowered himself on to his heels again. He was gazing at an empty cigarette packet, it was being turned in abrupt movements by the draught coming in the close. He wished he could get a pair of wide trousers. The mother and father were against them. He was lucky to get wearing long trousers at all. The father was having to wear short trousers and he was in his last year at school, just about ready to start serving his time at the trade. Boys nowadays were going to regret it for the rest of their days because they were being forced into long trousers before they needed to. Wide trousers. He wasn't bothered if he couldn't get the ones with the pockets down the sideseams, the ordinary ones would do.

The door of the pub swung open as a man came out and passed by the close. Danny was at the door. A hot draught of blue air and the smells of the drink, the whirr of the voices, reds and whites and blues and whites all laughing and swearing and chapping at dominoes.

He walked to the chip shop.

Ten number tens and a book of matches Mrs, for my da.

The woman gave him the cigarettes. When she gave his change he counted it slowly, he said: Much are your chips?

Same as the last time.

Will you give us a Milky Way, he asked.

He ate half of the chocolate and covered the rest with the wrapping, stuck it into his pocket. He smoked a cigarette; he got to his feet when he had tossed it away down the close.

Edging the door ajar he could see Uncle Archie still at the table. The beer was the same size as the last time. The small tumbler was going back to his lips. Danny sidled his way into the pub, but once inside he went quickly to the long table. He was holding the torn-in-half tickets for the return journey home, clenched in his right hand. He barged a way in between two men and put one of the tickets down on the table quite near to the beer glass.

I'm away now Uncle Archie.

What's up Danny boy?

Nothing. I'm just away home . . . He turned to go then said loudly: But I'll no tell my mother.

He pushed out through the men. He had to get out. Uncle Archie called after him but on he strode sidestepping his way beyond the crowded bar area.

Twenty minutes before the train would leave. In the waiting-room he sat by the door and watched for any sign of his uncle. It was quite quiet in the station, considering there had been a game during the afternoon. He found an empty section in a compartment of the train, closed the door and all of the windows, and opened the cigarette packet. The automatic doors shut. He stared back the way until the train had entered a bend in the track then stretched out, reaching his feet over on to the seat opposite. He closed his eyes. But had to open them immediately. He sat up straight, he dropped the cigarette on the floor and then lifted it up and opened the window to throw it out; he shut the window and sat down, resting his head on the back of the seat, he gazed at the floor. The train crashed on beneath the first bridge.

Eugenesis

WILLIAM MCILVANNEY

On the first day they eradicated war.
Nations were neutralized. In desert places
The cumbered void rusted with defused bombs,
The gutted chambers. In random heaps
The rockets lay, like molar monuments
To brontosauri sentenced to extinction.

On the second day They fed the starving.
The capsules gave immunity from hunger.
Faces filled. The smiles were uniform.
The computers had found a formula for plenty.

The third day ended work. With summer
Processed to a permanence, the sun-
Machine in operation, every day
Would be as long as They desired it.
Season-chambers were erected. The nostalgic
Could take a holiday to autumn if they wished.
The computers thought of everything.

On the fourth day death was dead.
Synthetic hearts, machine-tooled brains,
Eyes and limbs were all expendable.
Immortality came wrapped in polythene.
Every face was God's you saw upon the street.

By the fifth day crime was cured.
Mind-mechanics, They located every hatred,
Extracted it, and amputated angers.
Each idea was sterilized before its issue.
The computers fixed a safety-mark for thinking.

The sixth day saw heaven's inauguration.
Benignity pills were issued. Kindness meetings
Were held on every corner. They declared
Love as the prerogative of all.
That day became the longest there had been.
But as long as there was light the people smiled.

On the seventh day, while They were resting
A small man with red hair had disappeared.
A museum missed a tent. Neither was found.
He left an immortal wife, the changeless years
Of endless happiness, and a strange note
In ancient script, just four historic letters.
The Autotongue translated: 'Irrational Anger.'
The Medic Machine advised: 'Rejection Symptoms.
Source Unknown. Primordial and Contagious.'

It was too late. The word ran like a rash
On walls and daubed on doorways. Cities emptied.
In panic They neglected Their machines.
The sunset was unauthorized. Its beauty
Triggered the light-oriented metal cocks
That crew until their mechanisms burst.
Fires twinkled in the new night, shaping mattocks.
On the dark hills an unheavenly sound was heard.
The Historometer intoned into the silence:
'Ancient Barbaric Custom Known as Laughter.'
Seizing up, the computers began to cry.

Four of the Belt

TOM LEONARD

Jenkins, all too clearly it is time
for some ritual physical humiliation;
and if you cry, boy, you will prove
what I suspect – you are not a man.

As they say, Jenkins, this hurts me
more than it hurts you. But I show you
I am a man, by doing this, to you.

When *you* are a man, Jenkins, you may hear
that physical humiliation and ritual
are concerned with strange adult matters
– like rape, or masochistic fantasies.

You will not accept such stories.
Rather, you will recall with pride,
perhaps even affection, that day when I,
Mr Johnstone, summoned you before me,
and gave you four of the belt

like this. And this. And this. And this.

The Star

ALASDAIR GRAY

A star had fallen beyond the horizon, in Canada perhaps. (He had an aunt in Canada.) The second was nearer, just beyond the iron works, so he was not surprised when the third fell into the backyard. A flash of gold light lit the walls of the enclosing tenements and he heard a low musical chord. The light turned deep red and went out, and he knew that somewhere below a star was cooling in the night air. Turning from the window he saw that no one else had noticed. At the table his father, thoughtfully frowning, filled in a football coupon, his mother continued ironing under the pulley with its row of underwear. He said in a small voice, 'A'm gawn out.' His mother said, 'See you're no' long then.' He slipped through the lobby and on to the stairhead, banging the door after him.

The stairs were cold and coldly lit at each landing by a weak electric bulb. He hurried down three flights to the black silent yard and began hunting backward and forward, combing with his fingers the lank grass round the base of the clothes-pole. He found it in the midden on a decayed cabbage leaf. It was smooth and round, the size of a glass marble, and it shone with a light which made it seem to rest on a precious bit of green and yellow velvet. He picked it up. It was warm and filled his cupped palm with a ruby glow. He put it in his pocket and went back upstairs.

That night in bed he had a closer look. He slept with his

brother who was not easily wakened. Wriggling carefully far down under the sheets, he opened his palm and gazed. The star shone white and blue, making the space around him like a cave in an iceberg. He brought it close to his eye. In its depth was the pattern of a snowflake, the grandest thing he had ever seen. He looked through the flake's crystal lattice into an ocean of glittering blue-black waves under a sky full of huge galaxies. He heard a remote lulling sound like the sound in a sea shell, and fell asleep with the star safely clenched in his hand.

He enjoyed it for nearly two weeks, gazing at it each night below the sheets, sometimes seeing the snowflake, sometimes a flower, jewel, moon or landscape. At first he kept it hidden during the day but soon took to carrying it about with him; the smooth rounded gentle warmth in his pocket gave comfort when he felt insulted or neglected.

At school one afternoon he decided to take a quick look. He was at the back of the classroom in a desk by himself. The teacher was among the boys at the front row and all heads were bowed over books. Quickly he brought out the star and looked. It contained an aloof eye with a cool green pupil which dimmed and trembled as if seen through water.

'What have you there, Cameron?'

He shuddered and shut his hand.

'Marbles are for the playground, not the classroom. You'd better give it to me.'

'I cannae, sir.'

'I don't tolerate disobedience, Cameron. Give me that thing.'

The boy saw the teacher's face above him, the mouth opening and shutting under a clipped moustache. Suddenly he knew what to do and put the star in his mouth and swallowed. As the warmth sank toward his heart he felt relaxed and at ease. The teacher's face moved into the distance. Teacher, classroom, world receded like a rocket into a warm, easy blackness leaving behind a trail of glorious stars, and he was one of them.

Countdown

DAVE ANDERSON

Thursday night at 7.25
Some of them pose, some of them jive
It's a big fat 'Hey' from the cool DJ
With the winnin' way – what's he got to say?

It's a countdown
Top 30
Keep on rappin' (rappin', rappin')
30 in the charts is a bunch of farts
Tryin' to win your hearts, mimin' all the parts
29 is the funky kind
Every second line is feelin' fine
It's a genuine
Rappin'
Record

It's a countdown
Get down
Ooh-ah ooh-ah ooh-ah
Keep on rappin'
26 is a bunch of chicks
Legs akimbo
Doin' a limbo
Kinda rumba number
All about muscles

Macho men
Mucho muscles
How they love that stuff and can't get enough
Get down
And stay down
Seems to be what they got to say
A woman's place is on her back
Is what they chant to the backing track
Women's lib is just a fib
To these seductive
Counter productive
X-Certificate
Sex – Bombs
In the itty
Bitty
Teeny weeny pretty
Wrappin'
Get down and stay down
That's the way we like you
Get down and stay down
Keep you in your place

Back to the countdown
In with a bullet is a guy singin' cool it
And boogie for two and a half minutes dead
I'm no fool it won't win no Pulit-
zer prize. What the hell's goin' on in his head?

Get down
Number 20
What have we here?
It's a balladeer
With a seersucker shirt open down to here

And a vicious leer from ear to ear
He's a heart throb
Makes your heart throb with a kind of fear
Wants to hold you near
Call you dear
Seems so sincere but it's all veneer
Put a ring on your finger, bells on your toes
Give you a ring wherever he goes
Bells on your leg, pull the other one
He's an asshole
Sings a song
All about love
Wants you to
Go down

Meanwhile
Back to the countdown
At Number 16 is a teen-queen
Often seen on the cover of a magazine
She's a wet dream in skin tight jeans
Her production team is a mean machine
And she makes them scream and the song means
Nothin' at all
Never mind
She's a pop star

It's a countdown
Get down
Stay down
Keep on rappin'
Nothin'll happen
Meanwhile
There's another countdown goin' on
Maybe we should not dwell upon

Or should we?
Maybe, baby
There's a countdown gettin' awful near
Nothin' to do with what's goin' on here
Or has it?
You bet your ass it has
Young guns go for it
Big guns gonna get your ass
But your DJ with the winnin' way
Says 'hey!' guys and gals
Ooh-ah ooh-ah ooh-ah
As it happens
Keep on rappin'

It's a countdown
At Number 10 there's a mother hen
Lays eggs only for gentlemen
Sometimes nine, sometimes ten
Billion
Golden eggs
She's made a vow to the sacred cows
Of monetarism, capitalism
Freedmanism and jingoism
Sayin' rationalize, don't nationalize
Paralyse the wage rise
Prosecute the destitute
Pillorize the pensioner
Try to control the money supply
But don't control the money, honey
And don't forget the honey, Mummy
In the countdown
She's a real honey
Won't stop rappin'

What's next
In the countdown?
It's Numbers 10 and 11 together
Presentin' their version of Stormy Weather
It's Ye olde Thatcher and her prettier brother
Sayin' in unison
Can't get a place in Uni, son
Get down
Everybody
Get down and stay down
That's the way we like you
Stay down and pay up
While we step on your face

Comin' up fast is a blast from the past
Played way too fast by a cast of ghastly
Ghostly – white middle-class honky Rast-
Afarian
Aryans
Never mind the Ethiopian Utopian Dream
Babylonian nightmare
For the African
Check out the hairstyles

What about the countdown
Which one?
Number 5 million unemployed
Androids
In the void
Don't get annoyed, bank with Lloyds
And wait for it
The pick up

Meanwhile
Get down
Pick up your dole money, honey

Countdown
4 minutes to zero; Remember Nero?
Don't be a hero, forget your fear o'
Flyin' rockets – say sock it to me
Put your money in their pockets
And wait for it
It's gettin' closer
The countdown
Get down
Number 1
Don't forget Ronnie and American money
And his kinda frantic New Romantic
Paranoid schizoid Pretty-Boy-Floyd
Across the Atlantic Diplomacy

Don't forget the countdown
Which one?
The real one!
Rappin' till the break of dawn
Everybody
Get down
Duck –
And Good Luck!

Get down and stay down
That's the way we like you
Get down and stay down
Keep you in your place
Get down and stay down

That's the way we like you
Stay down and pay up
While we step on your face

True Story

JOAN URE

Here is another story that isn't a joke either. Because it's true. I was travelling in the bus on the way here and the pubs had just closed when a pink-faced man got on and sat down on the first seat he could find that had a space for him. He felt in his pocket for his money, then felt in the other pocket on the other side, bumping against the Jamaican who sat at the window side of the seat. He found his fare at last, counting it out carefully, sweat standing out on his forehead from the drink. He looked at his ticket then put it in his pocket, glanced at the Jamaican and murmured, then sat with his head flopped down on his chin as if he wanted to sleep. The bus stopped with a jerk and it wakened him up. He looked around. He and the Jamaican turned to face each other. The Jamaican smiled deprecatingly and turned away to look out of the window again. He had the *Guardian* on his knee. 'Why don't you read your paper, man,' the drunk, pink-faced man said, 'Don't mind me, read your paper, man.' 'Thank you,' the Jamaican said in a beautiful voice, 'but I've read it. Have it if you like.' 'Not me,' the sweating man said. 'Not me, not me.' He sat for a moment longer then, as if bracing himself, and accepting a challenge, he lifted his near arm heavily from his lap and put it around the Jamaican's neck. 'We're all the same, that's what I say, we're all of us the same, no matter what the colour of our skin – black, yellow or white.' The man's face was pinker than ever and the sweat streaked brown dust along its lines. The Jamaican smiled and nodded and said nothing.

The sweating pink-faced man hung on the Jamaican's neck, falling asleep and wakening at each jerk of the bus and when he saw where he hung, he'd say again in a voice that filled the whole of the bus, 'I don't hold with any of that colour bar stuff. I don't hold with it.' The sweat from his forehead must have been dripping on the Jamaican's white collar, but he sat patiently, looking out of the window. At last the drunk man lifted his arm away and looked full at the Jamaican, turning sideways in his seat to do it. 'You haven't heard a word I said, have you, man?' The Jamaican murmured, 'Oh yes, oh yes,' smiling rather sweetly. The drunk man said, 'No you haven't – you haven't been listening.' There was a silence and by now more people than myself were blushing at what we heard. What would happen now, we were all thinking. Then the Jamaican rose and said, 'Excuse me please, this is my stop.' 'What?' 'This is where I get out. This is where I live.' The whole bus waited, expecting the man to say, 'You don't want to sit beside me, do you man?' But it was all right. He really was a decent man – just clumsy and a bit insensitive. He got up and called to the conductor, 'Stop the bus. This gentleman wants to get off,' and he pulled at the hand rail in the ceiling, remembering the old days of the string bell.

After the Jamaican had left the bus, he looked around with his fists up – 'I don't hold with any of that colour bar stuff.' We were all of us quick to turn our heads away. I smiled to the Jamaican who was waiting to cross the road and at the sight of my smile, he burst out laughing. The whole bus was suddenly alight and we all began to laugh. The drunk man had fallen asleep curled up on the seat.

Initiation

WILLIAM MCILVANNEY

In shadowed and red-curtained room
My father talked towards his death
While birds made morning in the sky
And children laughed his death a lie
And each sun on the window-pane
Asked him would they meet again?

And I sat with him in the room,
Listened, nodded, laughed and talked
And brought him living words that mocked
The lonely, leafless road he walked.
He watched us distant, passing by.
Alone my father had to die.

Words withered in the barren breath.
Friends gathered in his lonely place,
Stood hope to hope and could not stop
Death closing on my father's face.
Love's bleeding fingers could not break
The way my father had to take.

Oh how time held us in his fist
And forced us to a helpless close,
Took a night, a room, a drifting mist
And nailed them on my father's life.

The cancer rotting in the lung
Cared not how many hands were wrung.

Then let me not take sackcloth for my grief
Or hang the hungry lashes with my tears.
This man went as quiet as a leaf,
Dumb as a lily in the singing years.
The wind in harebells will ring loud enough.
Nothing. Nothing. Nothing is enough.

Not the Burrell Collection

EDWIN MORGAN

The Buenos Aires Vase, one mile across,
flickering with unsleeping silent flames,
its marble carved in vine-leaves mixed with names,
shirtless ones and *desaparecidos*;
a collier's iron collar, riveted,
stamped by his Burntisland owner; a spade
from Babiy Yar; a blood-crust from the blade
that jumped the corpse of Wallace for his head;
the stout rack soaked in Machiavelli's sweat;
a fire-circled scorpion; a blown frog;
the siege of Beirut in stained glass; a sift
of Auschwitz ash; an old tapestry-set
unfinished, with a crowd, a witch, a log;
a lachrymatory no man can lift.

Saturday Song

MAUREEN MONAGHAN

He was about fourteen, clean, tidy and unlovely. Some sort of skin complaint, he was told; you'll grow out of it soon, he was promised. Meanwhile, he kept his boiled-looking face as much to himself as possible, and when he rubbed and scratched the raw cracks in his hands under his school desk, the teacher asked him what he was fidgeting with, and the other boys sniggered. Apart from scratching his hands, he seldom made any superfluous movements. So he was not kicking stones or crushing handfuls of the dusty hedge on that bright October morning. He just sat quietly on a low wall, clutching a small case and a cheap plastic folder under his arm. The wall faced the back of a row of crumbling houses, and the boy was staring absently at a broken window in the second house from the end.

An old man came slowly along the lane and into the yard. When he saw the boy, he stiffened, straightened his back and gathered his bulging string shopping bags close to him.

'What do you want?' He sounded weary. There was no answer. 'I said, what d'you want?' There was fear in the old man's voice.

There was a pause, then the boy said, 'Nothing. I'm just waiting.'

'Well you can't wait here. On your way, laddie!'

'No. I'll just stay. It's too early to go yet. I won't get in your way.' The boy spoke politely.

The old man almost mustered a roar, 'Move, son! I suppose it was your lot done that! Just get out of here and leave me in peace. Away home and break your own windows!'

'I'm sorry about your window,' said the boy, 'but I've just got here.' He stood up.

'I'm only waiting for a while, but I'll move along there if you like.'

He turned towards the old man, towards the other end of the shabby terrace, his mild blue eyes blinking and watering in the sun. There was no menace in him after all, no anger, except in the red blotchy skin. The old man sagged, too tired to argue any more. He handed over his bags and his keys as if to a neighbour of long standing. 'Will you carry the messages in for me, lad? They're heavier than I thought.'

The door opened into a narrow, stone-floored hallway smelly with paraffin cans, old newspapers and the passing attentions of cats. The boy had to squeeze himself against flaking, grey distemper to let the old man pass him and open the door half-way along the hall. A new set of smells and the twittering of a budgie greeted them as they entered the living-room.

The boy almost retched as the combined odours of bird-cage, bed and old age reached him. The old man, unnoticing, said, 'Come in, son. This is where I live. It's not very grand, but it does me fine. Could you put some coal on? It's a bit cold.'

He sank into a worn, lumpy armchair. The boy put the string bags on the table and laid down his own case and folder too. He looked around for tongs or a shovel, then used his hands, reluctantly.

'Who's C.P.M.?'

The boy turned, startled. The old man was looking at the

case. 'Oh, that was my Dad, Colin Peter Morrison. I'm just Peter.'

'Your Dad's passed on, then? What's in the case?'

'Nothing. A clarinet. It was my Dad's.'

The old man looked eager. 'Can you play it?'

'No!'

'Not even a wee bit?'

'No. I hate it!'

'Are you learning to play it?'

'No. My Mum sent me to lessons. But I hate it. Can I wash my hands?'

'Over there. Why d'you hate it?'

But Peter turned on the tap and washed his hands carefully. Then since the water was hot, he wiped out the greasy sink and started to wash the dishes which were in the sink, beside the sink, on the table and on the mantelpiece. He wet an old cloth which was bundled on the wooden draining-board, and washed off the ash and coal-dust and tea stains from the hearth. He looked at the filthy cloth.

'I think I should just throw this away now.'

'Aye! You're a tidy fellow. D'you like the bird? Her name's Jinty. She's good company.'

'Uh-huh. My Dad used to keep birds, but my Mum never liked them. I could clean out the cage. Does she get out?'

'She'll not go far. She likes the mantelpiece.'

Peter opened the cage door with the bird trying to peck his fingers. It fluttered on to the old man's head, flew over to one of the square, varnished bedposts and finally settled on the brightly painted toffee-tin above the fireplace, squawking quietly.

The old man said soothingly, 'Sssh, beauty, sssh! He's just making your house nice. He'll not hurt you.'

Peter crossed to the sink to fill the little water bowl. 'Where d'you keep the birdseed?'

'Here, I've just bought some more. She'll soon get used to you.' He hesitated, then added, 'She'll know you next time.'

'Mr Briggs, could I . . . ?'

'How d'you know my name?' the old man asked sharply.

'Your pension book. It's on the mantelpiece. It's just a different colour from my Mum's.'

'Don't miss much, do you, son?' he mumbled.

'Mr Briggs, I could come for a while on Saturdays, and . . . and help you. You know, clean up a bit, or go to the shops. I haven't . . . I mean, there's nothing else to do.' Peter held his finger out to the budgie. The bird ignored him, flew back to the cage and warbled at its reflection in the tiny mirror. 'Would you like me to wash the window? I've still got time.'

'Leave it, lad. You can do it next week.'

Peter shut the door of the birdcage. 'Oh! Fine! I'll come about ten.'

'That'll be nice.' The old man's gaze was resting on the clarinet case. 'Why d'you hate it?'

'What? Oh! I just do.'

'Play us a tune.'

'No! I've told you! I can't. I'll need to go now.' The red patches glowed on Peter's face and neck.

'What were you waiting for, son?'

'Nothing. It doesn't matter.' Behind his back he rubbed his itching hands against his trousers, against each other. 'Will I come next Saturday then?'

He tucked the clarinet and the folder under his arm. The old man was running his thumb-nail back and forward over the top of the birdcage. 'What d'you think, Jinty? Will we let him come back? Maybe he'll give us a tune next time.'

The bird cocked its head, first to one side, then to the other. Peter opened the door into the damp hallway.

'Jinty says you can come. You could wait at the end of the lane and carry the messages. If you want to.'

Peter's fiery skin began to cool. 'Right! Cheerio! See you on Saturday, Mr Briggs.'

'Shut the doors behind you, son!'

Peter shut the living-room door. Going down the hall, he added shyly, 'Cheerio, Jinty.'

Their Saturday mornings settled into an easy routine. Peter, always with the clarinet and music-folder under his arm, would meet Mr Briggs outside the corner shop. The old man would hand over his bags and they would walk slowly, companionably, along the lane which became barer and muddier as the weeks went on. Once inside the house, the boy would fill the coal buckets while the old man made tea. They would drink it in front of the fire and slip cake crumbs to the budgie through the bars of the cage. Then Peter would gather up everything that looked like rubbish, take it out to the dustbin and push an ancient, rattling sweeper over the thin carpet. He would clean out the birdcage, and wash the window, if it wasn't raining. Mr Briggs would potter around, put away his meagre groceries, start to peel potatoes, then abandon them in favour of another mug of stewed tea.

The conversation was hardly more varied than the housework.

'And how's the school, lad?'

'Fine.'

'Doing all right then?'

'Uh-huh.'

'You mind and stick in. I wish I had.'

'Uh-huh.'

Peter would brace himself for the next bit.

'How about a wee tune, then? Me and Jinty would like a wee tune. Wouldn't we, beauty?' The bird would trill obligingly.

Sometimes the old man held out the clarinet case towards the boy. Sometimes he would open it and stroke the red plush lining, or run his finger along the dark, shiny wood. 'C'mon son. Play us a tune.'

'No! I can't.'

'Aw, you could if you tried.'

'I don't want to!'

Mr Briggs would shake his head, sigh loudly and return to his potato peeling, looking hurt. Eventually he would say, 'Is there time for more tea?'

And Peter would look at his watch, pick up his things and say, 'No. I'd better be going. Will I come again next week?'

They would both look round the hot, tidy room.

'Aye, laddie. See you next Saturday.'

The last Saturday in November was wild and stormy. Peter was already soaked by the time Mr Briggs came out of the shop with his usual string bags tucked inside plastic carriers. They ploughed along the filthy lane, heads down against the rain, bumping into each other as they fought the wind. The old man kept tugging at his hat and pulling up his coat collar, but Peter had the shopping in one hand and the clarinet and music-case in the other, and the rain dribbled unchecked round his neck and wrists.

'It's a dirty day, all right,' said Mr Briggs, sounding quite cheerful. 'I wondered if you'd bother coming.'

'I said I would.' The carrier-bags cut into Peter's hand, and he thought he might drop something.

'You're a good lad. We'll soon be home. The fire should be just nice when we get in.'

They turned into the yard and the wind blew the bags against Peter's wet legs as he struggled across the path to the door. When the door was opened, Peter almost fell into the hallway. He hurried into the stuffy, fetid living-room and dropped everything in a heap on the table. His hands were aching with cold, and he stood about miserably while Mr Briggs hung up his coat and hat, and filled the kettle.

'Get that wet jacket off you, son. You'll maybe have to stay a bit longer, till it dries. I'll make the tea. You sit and warm yourself.'

Peter took off his anorak and bundled it over the back of a chair. The old man had poked the fire and put pieces of coal round it without spoiling its blazing heart. Peter held out his hands to it, knowing that he should have rubbed his dripping hair and patted the wet cracks between his fingers. Already he could feel his face becoming taut in the dry heat. He crossed to the sink, let the water run for a minute, then put the stopper in. 'I'd better get busy. There's a lot to do.'

Mr Briggs reached from behind him and turned off the tap. 'Nothing that won't wait, laddie. Come away from there. Just sit down, like I said, and get this tea inside you.'

Peter sat in one of the fireside chairs with his hands wrapped round the steaming mug. Mr Briggs brought a plate of sticky buns and put it on the hearth near the boy.

'Mind and save some bits for Jinty. I'll let her out for a wee flutter.' He opened the cage, but the bird remained on its perch, singing ecstatically. He looked at the budgie fondly.

'She likes when it's raining. She knows fine we'll not rush off and leave her.'

He held out a piece of his bun into the cage. The bird

pecked it out of his fingers, dropped it and went on singing. 'Cheeky thing!' he said indulgently.

Peter started to drink his tea. His face was burning, and between mouthfuls of tea and bun he hunched up first one shoulder, then the other, and rubbed the flaming patches on his cheeks against his rough sweater.

'What's wrong lad?'

'Nothing.'

'You don't look right. What's wrong with your face?'

'Nothing!'

Before the old man could ask any more questions, the bird flew out of the cage and rested for a moment on Peter's head on its way to the mantelpiece. The old man was delighted. 'Oh, I knew she'd get used to you! She likes you! You'll not get rid of her next week!'

'I won't be here next week,' said Peter quietly.

'What? Why not?'

'I can't come. I won't be coming again. I'll just tidy up a bit now. Maybe during the holidays . . . ,' he said half-heartedly, while rubbing his itching hands on his trousers. He brought the carpet-sweeper out from the cupboard in the wall and pushed it around the middle of the room. Mr Briggs kept getting in the way.

'Why can't you come? Why did you come in the first place?'

'It doesn't matter.'

Peter left the sweeper standing, took a duster from under the sink and swept it smartly along the mantelpiece. The startled bird swooped round the room three times before heading for the cage. Peter's hand reached the cage door first.

'No you don't! I'm going to clean your cage properly – and you keep it clean!'

The bird sat on top of the cage looking puzzled.

'Just leave it, son. She's tired. Leave it till next week.'

'I told you! I won't be back!'

'You haven't told me much. Why are you here?'

Peter ignored him. 'I'll just give her clean water,' he said, taking the plastic bowl to the tap. The bird scrambled into the cage, and the boy replaced the bowl and shut the door.

'You should be up at the school, shouldn't you?' The old man was jubilant when he saw the change in Peter's face. 'Shouldn't you?'

'No!'

'I heard about those music lessons. Trumpets and flutes and violins. All sorts of things. And clarinets!' he added triumphantly.

'I don't have to go!'

'Aye, but that's where your Ma thinks you've gone! Isn't it?' He lifted the clarinet case from the table and thrust it under Peter's nose. The boy turned his head away.

'What happened son? Why can't you come next week? Did someone tell on you?'

'No! But I can't come back.'

Peter busied himself at the sink. He thought of all the excuses he had already given his music teacher. He thought of all the other excuses he had stored up ready, but which he could not now use because his music teacher had stopped believing him. At least he could blame the weather this week. He heard Mr Briggs opening the catches of the case and waited for the dreaded wheedling words.

'We'll surely get a tune this time, Jinty. He couldn't leave us without a tune!'

Peter clashed the dishes in the soapy water. He pulled out the stopper and piled them on the draining-board.

'C'mon son. You know how much we want to hear you play! We don't mind if you're not very good!'

Peter half-dried his sore, raw hands. He took his anorak from the chair near the fire and put it on. It steamed with his body's heat. He started to tidy the bags he had dumped on the table, first laying his music-folder on one side.

'Maybe he can't play at all, Jinty! Maybe he just carries that case because it looks nice! If he doesn't play us a tune this time, we'll never know, will we?'

The itch between Peter's fingers was unbearable. He rushed the sweeper across the room and jammed it into a corner. 'All right! All right!'

He snatched the case from the old man's hands and banged it down on the table. Deftly, he screwed the sections of the clarinet together, lining up the keys as if it was the habit of a lifetime. He took the protective metal cap off the mouthpiece, sucked the reed before positioning it and tightened the silver ligature which kept it in place. Mr Briggs was fascinated by the busy, skilful hands. He only noticed the boy's grim face when it glared redly a few inches from his own. He shrank back into his armchair.

Peter hissed at him, 'I'll give you a tune! And your stupid bird as well! You've asked for it. You'll be sorry. Here's a tune for you!'

He stuck the clarinet angrily in his mouth and blasted hard, crude notes at the old man, repeating the vulgar theme over and over like a cruel, taunting child.

Hands to his ears, Mr Briggs whimpered, 'Stop it! Oh, stop it, lad! It doesn't matter about the tune. You're frightening the bird!'

The terrified budgie was screeching and flapping, banging itself off the sides of the cage, scattering birdseed and water and tiny green feathers through the bars. Peter turned away from the old man. He blew long, unpitched rasps towards the bird, holding the clarinet in one hand while he opened the cage door with the other. He pushed the bell of the instrument into the cage, crouching level with the table on which it stood. The little quivering creature scrambled dementedly between floor and perch. It puffed out its heaving breast as if to push away the vicious, insistent tune. Mr Briggs stumbled over from his chair and pummelled Peter with his old soft fists, pleading and sobbing.

The bird was suddenly calm. It chirped once, and keeled over on its side at the bottom of the cage, one tiny eye staring beadily upwards. It gave a gentle shudder, then lay still. Peter stared in horror at the dead bird.

The old man wailed, 'You've killed her! You wee bugger! You wicked wee bugger! You've killed Jinty! Oh, the poor bird! You've killed her!'

The boy pulled the clarinet roughly out of the cage and ran out of the room and down the hallway, with the cries ringing in his ears. He ran across the yard and along the lane, ran all the way home in the driving, sleety rain. At last he stood, dripping and panting, on his doorstep and fumbled for his key. At some point he must have put the instrument inside his anorak for protection, and he realized, as his fingers touched the clammy wood, that he had left the clarinet-case behind.

The wind had died and the rain was a fine drizzle when Peter went back to the house after school on Monday. He crossed the muddy yard and was relieved to find the front door unlocked and swinging slightly in the breeze. Rain had blown into the hallway. There was no rush of warmth from the living-room as he opened the door. The fire was out, a

heap of fine ash spilling over on to the hearth, and the usual
smells were suspended in the chill air.

The birdcage was shrouded in its flowered night-time
cover. Mr Briggs lay back in his armchair, his legs stretched
stiffly in front of him, his mouth open. Peter was surprised
that he was not snoring. He called his name softly. Then,
since there was no answer, he tiptoed to the cluttered table
and gathered up his case and his music-folder. 'Cheerio, Mr
Briggs,' he said quietly. He left the cold, silent house,
shutting the door behind him.

After his tea he went upstairs to his bedroom. He assem-
bled the instrument and propped up 'Daily Exercises for the
Clarinet Student' on the bookshelf. He started to practise. A
family of starlings chattered and complained outside his
window. Before long his eyes were filled with tears and he
had to stop to blow his nose. He started playing again. The
third time the music came to a sort of gurgling halt, his
mother wondered downstairs if perhaps the clarinet lessons
were a waste of time.

Vymura: the Shade Card Poem

LIZ LOCHHEAD

Now artistic I aint, but I went to choose paint
'cos the state of the place made me sick.
I got a shade card, consumers'-aid card, but it stayed hard
   to pick
So I asked her advice as to what would look nice,
would blend in and not get on my wick.

She said 'Our Vymura is super in Dürer,
or see what you think of this new shade, Vlaminck.
But I see that you're choosy . . .
Picasso is newsy . . . that's greyish-greeny-bluesy . . .
Derain's all the rage . . .
that's hot-pink and Fauve-ish . . .
There's Monet . . . that's mauve-ish . . .
And Schwitters,
that's sort-of-a *beige*.'

She said 'Fellow next door just sanded his floor
and rollered on Rouault and Rothko
His hall, och it's Pollock an' he
did his lounge in soft Hockney
with his cornice picked out in Kokoshka.'

'Now avoid the Van Gogh, you'll not get it off,
the Bonnard is bonny,

you'd be safe with matt Manet,
the Goya is *gorgeous*
or Chagall in eggshell,
but full-gloss Lautrec's sort of tacky.
So stick if you can to satin-finish Cézanne
or Constable . . . that's kind of khaki.
Or the Gainsborough green . . .
and I'd call it hooey to say Cimabue
would never tone in with Soutine.'

'If it looks a bit narrow when you splash on Pissarro,
one-coat Magritte covers over.'
She said 'This Hitchens is a nice shade for kitchens
with some Ernst to connect 'em at other end of the
    spectrum
Botticelli's lovely in the Louvre.'
She said 'If it was mine I'd do it Jim Dine . . .
don't think me élitist or snobby . . .
but Filipo Lippi'd
look awfy inspid,
especially in a large-ish lobby!'

Well, I did one wall Watteau, with the skirting Giotto
and the door and the pelmet in Poussin.
The ceiling's de Kooning,
other walls all in Hals
and the whole place looks quite . . . cavalier,
with the woodwork in Corot –
but I think tomorrow
I'll flat-white it back to Vermeer.

Acknowledgements

The editors and publishers wish to thank the following for permission to use copyright material in this collection:

Keith Aitchison and William Collins Ltd for 'Blood' in *Scottish Short Stories* (annual); Dave Anderson for 'Countdown'; Edward Boyle and Workers Educational Association (West of Scotland District) for 'The Great McGunnigle'; Douglas Dunn and Faber and Faber Ltd for 'After the War' in *The Happier Life* and 'Washing the Coins' in *St Kilda's Parliament*; Alasdair Gray for 'The Star' in *Unlikely Stories Mostly*, Canongate; James Kelman for 'Away in Airdrie' in *Not Not While the Giro*, Polygon; Tom Leonard for 'Four of the Belt' and 'Moral Philosophy' in *Intimate Voices*, Galloping Dog Press; Liz Lochhead for 'Two Birds' in *Dreaming Frankenstein*, Polygon, and 'Fat Girl's Confession', 'Vymura the Shade Card Poem' in *True Confessions*, Polygon; William McIlvanney and J. Farqharson Ltd for 'Eugenesis' and 'Initiation' in *Longships in Harbour*; Adam McNaughtan for 'Oor Hamlet'; Maureen Monaghan for 'Saturday Song'; Edwin Morgan and Carcanet Ltd for 'At Central Station' in *Poems of Thirty Years*, Mariscat Press for 'Not the Burrell Collection' in *Sonnets from Scotland*, and 'Glasgow October 1972', 'Brisbane November 1972', 'London August 1972' in *Takes and Grafts*; Alan Spence and Salamander Press for 'The Ferry' (adapted) in *It's Colours They Are Fine* Salamander/Corgi; Liam Stewart for 'A Picture of Zoe'; Geddes Thomson for 'The New Boy'; John Carswell for 'True Story' by Joan Ure; Arthur Young and William Collins Ltd for 'The Staff of Life' in *Scottish Short Stories* (annual).